TO BE A SOLDIER

Excerpts from an imagined WW2 diary

RICHARD BEMAND

TO BE A
SOLDIER

Excerpts from an imagined WW2 diary

RICHARD BEMAND

MEREO
Cirencester

Mereo Books

1A The Wool Market Dyer Street Cirencester Gloucestershire GL7 2PR
An imprint of Memoirs Publishing www.mereobooks.com

To be a soldier: 978-1-86151-667-1

First published in Great Britain in 2016
by Mereo Books, an imprint of Memoirs Publishing

The address for Memoirs Publishing Group Limited can be found at
www.memoirspublishing.com

The Memoirs Publishing Group Ltd Reg. No. 7834348

The Memoirs Publishing Group supports both The Forest Stewardship Council®
(FSC®) and the PEFC® leading international forest-certification organisations. Our
books carrying both the FSC label and the PEFC® and are printed on FSC®-certified
paper. FSC® is the only forest-certification scheme supported by the leading
environmental organisations including Greenpeace. Our paper procurement policy
can be found at www.memoirspublishing.com/environment

Typeset in 10/15pt Century Schoolbook
by Wiltshire Associates Publisher Services Ltd. Printed and bound in Great Britain
by Printondemand-Worldwide, Peterborough PE2 6XD

INTRODUCTION

In 2015 we celebrated the 70th Anniversary of the end of the Second World War. This book is based on an imaginary diary written by a Christian soldier in World War II, from the opening of hostilities in 1939 to the end of the war in 1945. The accounts of events it covers are based on fact but, as in any military force, rumours and speculation abound from day to day. At times our soldier seeks to add a touch of light-hearted humour, sometimes necessary to sustain morale. The soldier's diary looks at some of these events, together with thoughts about his family and personal life at the time, and reflects on the events of the war as they relate to his Christian life.

Dedicated to my father, RAF Sergeant
Robert Eric Bemand, who served in Malta during WW2.

1939

1

TENSION MOUNTS

Thursday 31st August 1939

All around the country there is concern. When Prime Minister Neville Chamberlain flew back from Munich he was waving his piece of paper and announced confidently "Peace in our time". Many people believed that war had been avoided, but at a price. Hitler's demands for territory in Czechoslovakia had been granted, if reluctantly, but there was always the worry that he wouldn't stop there, and that he might make further territorial demands that would be impossible to meet. What would happen next? The attitude is cautious, but it is still thought that should Germany make any move involving military forces, then we would certainly match them.

Earlier this month my wife Julie and I celebrated our sixth wedding anniversary. I had known Julie before simply as a special school friend, but after she moved with her parents to North London we always kept in touch by letter. I called to see her again whilst on a visit to London, and our feelings for each other had not changed. We married in 1933, and our son Bobby was born in May 1935.

We live in Sussex, so Julie and I went to the local church service near Worthing last week that we attend regularly, and there were many who prayed for peace. The minister himself brought us all together towards the end of the service and led all the prayers. We usually have a weekly meeting at home, so the same has been done during our fellowship times. That is the first step, but God answers prayer in His own way and not necessarily in the way we may expect. Jesus already knew what lay ahead when he went to the Garden of Gethsemane to pray, so he told the disciples who had come with him "My soul is overwhelmed with sorrow to the point of death. Stay here and keep watch with me" (Matthew 26:38). He then went on to pray "My Father, if it is possible, may this cup be taken from me. Yet not as I will, but as you will" (v.39). Jesus knew that his Father God was supreme, and if he were to bear the heavy burden of mankind's sin upon his shoulders on the cross at Calvary, then it would only be possible through his complete obedience to God. Even so, he prayed a second time: "My Father, if it is not possible for this cup to be taken away unless I drink it, may your will be done" (v.42), and a third time as well. It was to be a heavy burden indeed, but Jesus was declaring his commitment to abide by what God wanted, and not what he wanted.

2

IN THE BEGINNING

Saturday 30th September 1939

Gas masks are being distributed everywhere, and at home we are taking a few other precautions as well. The Civil Defence is creating a few thickly-padded air raid shelters, and some of the neighbours are almost entrenching themselves in their gardens trying to build their own shelters from brick and corrugated iron, though until they have sandbags on top of them they won't look too sturdy. We've managed to get hold of some sticky tape and card to paste over our windows. If anything does happen, then that should help.

Then, on the first day of this month, the German forces suddenly and without warning invaded Poland. They were filmed enthusiastically opening the border gates and commencing hostilities against the Polish army. Two days later, on 3rd September, and at about 11 o'clock in the morning, we listened to Chamberlain announcing that there had been no response to the ultimatum for Hitler's army to withdraw from Poland and that 'This country is at war with Germany'. Soon afterwards the air raid warning wailed out and everyone ran for cover, though it was a false alarm. Even newsboys have been scurrying around with sandwich boards showing 'War Declared - Official'.

Morale is high and it is said that the war will be all over by Christmas, but I'm not so sure. Very few have any real idea what we will be up against. Let's not forget that the Germans already have plenty of combat experience from the Spanish Civil War, when Hitler offered their services to the Spanish dictator, General Franco.

I see it just like our lives as Christians. We can take a step of faith and state our belief in the Lord Jesus Christ, but it doesn't stop there. Throughout our lives we may undertake the tasks that God has given us, but we should remember that in the background we could also face trials and temptations, just as Jesus did himself. Let's be ready to face whatever Satan throws at us. Right through the Bible, in both the Old Testament and the New Testament, there are instances where God's strength is remarked upon. When David became King of Israel, he reclaimed the Ark of the Covenant and brought it back to Jerusalem. In his giving thanks, David says "Look to the Lord and his strength; seek his face always. Remember the wonders he has done, his miracles, and the judgements he pronounced" (1 Chronicles 16:11-12). The apostle Paul, in his letter to the new church at Corinth, writes "For the foolishness of God is wiser than men's wisdom, and the weakness of God is stronger than man's strength" (1 Cor. 1:25). To win not only the battles, but the war that has come upon us, what more strength could we, as loyal Christians, ask for?

3

WHICH SIDE ARE YOU ON?

Tuesday 31st October 1939

There have been reports of fascist marches led by Oswald Mosley and his so-called blackshirts trying to raise support for the Nazi cause, not only in this country but abroad as well. Our neighbours detest this activity, and are forming a local group to make sure that nothing like that happens in our town. In London I became involved in a group of demonstrators who had been tipped off that a march was due to take place. Whilst the police tried to create a passage for the marchers, the demonstrators put up obstructions of every sort to stop them. There are still politicians who claim that to make peace with Germany would be a lot more beneficial than keeping up hostilities. So many have been misled by all these false promises, either because they are unaware of or do not believe reports of the oppression that has been carried out in Germany against anyone who disagrees with the Nazi policy, together with groups like gypsies, who are considered unwelcome. Not only that, but much of the territory that Hitler has forcibly occupied has also been set aflame.

Before I became a Christian I was told that I had this hereditary disease called sin, and that those infected with it were likely to end up in a big fire! When asked what the cure was, I was told that it was important to accept the rule and authority of Jesus Christ, the Son of God, in my life. I was told how Jesus was the doctor who could heal me, because He had already removed the sin virus from all who believed in Him when He died upon the cross at Calvary, and that God cared so much for us that He didn't want us to die, but to have eternal life (John 3:16). In the Bible I also read that God already has victory in His hands, and of what would subsequently happen to all His enemies (1 Cor. 15:26-26).

Everything has been so difficult to take in. I'm afraid, and there's no doubt about it. But the vital question still stands: "Which side are you on?"

4

WHICH SIDE ARE YOU ON?

Thursday 30th November 1939

Earlier this week I decided to sign up for the military forces. It wasn't an easy decision, and the family were in two minds about it. My father-in-law Charles, who had fought in the Great War, was eager for me to enlist, but I know my wife has fears for my safety, and stressed the fact that I would be leaving my young son Bobby. Nevertheless, it was the one decision that I had to make. Only by doing this did I feel

I would be doing my duty towards King and Country.

There have been queues of men lining up, but I was too cautious to go straight in immediately. Charles has spoken to me of the excitement that he felt as a new recruit whilst thinking of the new adventure that lay ahead. He then told me of how that myth vanished once he entered into combat. A soldier suddenly becomes aware of the dangers around, and that excitement is replaced by a strange feeling of uneasy wariness that can lead to him being trigger-happy. When orders are received, they are carried out without question, whether we agree with them or not. We are there to do a job, not to organize a gossip group to examine everything in detail.

Even so, I was quite puzzled when I was offered a commission almost immediately. I worked out that during the enlistment process I would be asked about my religious beliefs, so I stated quite openly that I was a committed Christian. Having become a little irritated by the time it took to get everything worked out, I then looked over quite sternly towards the young private on the other side of the desk and asked "Why do you not salute? I am a captain in the Army!" I was of course referring to my rank in the Salvation Army, with which I had had links for several years. All round Worthing the SA sought to help some of the old soldiers still suffering from the trauma of the Great War, as well as everyday folk who had simply fallen on hard times.

The private looked startled, then hurriedly stood to attention. Even though I had never been taught how to salute correctly, I was familiar with all the usual commands in the British Army, so I returned his salute in quite a leisurely fashion and told him to stand easy, because I was only wearing civilian clothes. The unexpected commission does mean that I will get an extra bath in the officers' quarters every week!

At the time it reminded me of when I became a Christian. When I asked how I should sign up in God's army I received the not exactly courteous reply that I should have realized that I didn't have to put my name down in writing anywhere, but just to truly believe in the Lord Jesus Christ (ref. Acts 16:30). I would need to repent of my sin and then, just as Jesus himself was, be baptised as a sign of my new commitment to God, my intention to follow in His way, and to seek to grow in my understanding of His Truth through the Holy Spirit abiding within me. When this happened, it was said, my name would be automatically written in God's own heavenly book.

I realize that not everything will be easy, and no doubt there will be times when a price has to be paid. If I had expected an easy road to heaven then I was certainly mistaken, and standards will need to be kept. I read soon after that "Nothing impure will ever enter (heaven), nor will anyone who does what is shameful or deceitful, but only those whose names are written in the Lamb's book of life" (Rev. 21:27). For me the choice is clear - DEATH on one side or GLORY, regardless of the cost, on the other - and I've no intention of missing out!

5

BEWARE THE WOLVES!

Sunday 31st December 1939

There was much news about the sinking of the enemy pocket battleship *Admiral Graf Spee* in Montevideo harbour. The news was that she had already sunk nine of our merchant ships in the Atlantic, so it was essential that something was done. We had three cruisers in the area that were patrolling in search of Hitler's surface raider, the *Ajax*, *Achilles* and *Exeter*. They attacked almost as soon as the lookouts spotted her, and gained the advantage by attacking from two sides, which meant that the *Graf Spee* couldn't bring all her main armament to bear on one ship alone.

The *Exeter* took heavy damage, and it is believed that the ship's captain, whose ship was still undergoing some repair work, sent a radio message to the commander on board the *Ajax* requesting "a revised list of spares". However, the *Graf Spee* also took heavy damage, and put into the port of Montevideo in neutral Uruguay to make repairs. Captain Lindemann, on board the enemy battleship, must have received intelligence reports stating that we had a number of warships, including a couple of battleships, waiting in the mouth of the River Plate for when *Graf Spee* left Montevideo harbour. Having only had 72 hours to make his ship seaworthy again, and in view of the fact that he would have had no chance against all the guns that he believed were waiting for him, he preferred to scuttle the ship soon after it got under way with a bare minimum of crew left on board. The crews of the three cruisers have been treated like heroes.

Unfortunately we were never told much about the sinking of our own battleship, HMS *Royal Oak*, back in October. It was said that Gunther Prien, the commander of the enemy submarine U47, followed undetected in the wake of a British minesweeper right into Scapa Flow, where the Home Fleet was harboured. No wonder they have described their submarines as 'sea wolves'.

I was given a 48-hour leave pass by our CO, and spent Christmas with the family near Worthing. So far they seem to be managing quite well, but I think they need to keep a small food reserve in the kitchen if there are any severe restrictions.

I love playing hide and seek in our garden with Bobby. He's still small, so he can hide in one place, then secretly move to where I had just looked. It often takes ages to find him. I wonder if the submarine captains think like that. They can move so stealthily that it can be hard to find them. One tactic they are using is to hide underneath the searching destroyer or any other suitable ship. Our detection equipment uses sound waves to find the submarine, so if it is under another ship then the sound waves may only register the presence of one ship, and the submarine may remain undetected.

I think it's like that in our Christian lives. Once we're in what we believe to be a safe haven, we don't consider that anyone can touch us. But Jesus always showed his disciples that wherever they were, they should beware of those who try to deter us. Right from the beginning of time, and throughout the Bible, there have been stories of those who had been blessed by God, then turned away from Him. The very first example of this is in the story of Adam and Eve in the Garden of Eden. Both of them were taken in by the serpent, who was described as "more crafty than any of the wild animals the Lord God had made" (Genesis 3:1). God banished them from the garden after they had eaten the fruit of the Tree of the Knowledge of Good and Evil. Satan, who is that same serpent in our lives today, has many powers in this world, like mischief and deceit, so as Christians let's make sure we are aware of this. We can make sure we're walking along the straight and narrow Christian path, but let's never forget to look over our shoulders to make sure we're not attacked from behind.

6
DID I SAY ACTION?

Wednesday 31st January 1940

When I joined the forces I thought I might see action and become some sort of hero on the battlefield. I was mistaken. For weeks I must have done more marching up and down and round and round than Joshua and all the priests who marched round Jericho. The only combat experience we have had for the moment has been learning how to stick straw dummies with bayonets! However, we have now been shipped over to the French border to join the British Expeditionary Force (BEF).

This last month has been so quiet, and we're trying to keep busy to try and beat the cold weather. We could do with something a bit thicker than cloaks or thin trench coats. It's as if many are expecting the same type of trench warfare that their fathers saw in the Great War. Everything seems quiet on the Western Front, but I hope we don't get over-confident. There is a kind of uneasiness around, and it's almost too quiet for comfort.

Last Christmas there was so much snow on the ground at home that I took Bobby outside to build a big snowman. If it's as cold back at home as it is here in France then I expect the snowman's still outside now, but I don't expect he's waiting for the sun to come out!

Even so, it reminds me of Paul's letters to the young evangelist Timothy, in which Paul seeks to instruct and enlighten him in many ways. He also warns Timothy of the consequences of ignoring the teaching of the Holy Spirit and gives particular examples of this (see 1 Tim. 1:18-20). The consequence is similar to what we read in the book of Hebrews, "We must pay more attention, therefore, to what we have heard, so that we do not drift away. For if the message spoken by angels was binding, and every violation and disobedience received its just punishment, how shall we escape if we ignore such a great salvation?" (Heb. 2:1-3)

The task now seems quite daunting, but I'm still facing

the fact that there are very few weapons around yet. I wonder where they are?

7

RESCUED!

Thursday 29th February 1940

We are told that British warships with Royal Marines on board have sailed into Norwegian waters to rescue sailors imprisoned on the German merchant ship *Altmark*. We know that this ship had been in the South Atlantic for three months, supplying the pocket battleship *Graf Spee* with fuel, oil and other supplies. The sailors whom we rescued came from some of the ships that were sunk by the *Graf Spee* before its demise in Montevideo harbour last December. The *Altmark* must have returned to Norway recently, either in order to resupply ready to go out again to act as a supply ship for the enemy surface raiders or, more likely, to pass through Norwegian waters on its way back to Germany for repairs. Being a neutral country, the Norwegians sent one of their naval officers to check the ship, which would be standard procedure, but the *Altmark*'s captain claimed she was an unarmed tanker. Though they were possibly made aware that the ship was carrying some prisoners, the impression is that she was cleared because of the Norwegians' fear of any retaliation by Germany. The Norwegian government maintains its neutrality and has objected to the incident.

My sergeant-major is keeping everyone on their toes. He's the sort who keeps a close eye on everything and always objects if anyone does something that is, according to him, not in the army rule book. However petty the incident, he will certainly let me know about it! Still, I can't really complain, because the standard of discipline he maintains is excellent.

It can be like that with Christians sometimes, and especially missionaries. In one country the population will be welcoming, but in another there are those who object to the presence of Christians, even though their one desire is to help others and rescue them from the enslavement that sin brings about. The uncertainty in the atmosphere is hard to put up with. Even at home Christians are sometimes looked upon with suspicion. Our faith in Jesus Christ, and the fact that we can practise what we preach in our daily lives, will help. However, we all have to rely on Jesus for our strength.

8

DIG FOR VICTORY

Sunday 31st March 1940

Last week I had a long letter from my Julie, telling me how everyone is coping with rationing. Our family is just one of those beginning to feel the cutbacks that we've all had to make since this war started. They started rationing last January with cutbacks on items like butter and bacon. Now meat rationing has started. We have all been given new ration books with the coupons that shopkeepers remove each time we make a purchase, but we will still have to find other ways to produce meals. When Julie and I visited him last Christmas, my father Edward, who lives out in the country now, served up some dandelion tea, and even suggested that we try the old recipe for nettle soup. I think it tastes awful, but if that's all one can get then I suppose it's always worthwhile trying. Julie says that Bobby also misses his slice of cheese, and one egg per week is hard for them both. I've suggested that they keep a couple of hens in the back garden.

We've been quite lucky, living near a river. My son bought a fishing rod and has been given several tips in the skill of angling. There is still a black market trade in illegal foods, and it appears that one lady from London was fined

£75 recently for having hoarded 140 weeks' ration of sugar.

The new street poster invites everyone to 'Dig For Victory' and help grow their own food. Everyone seems to have got the message, because many areas that were once lawns are now being cultivated, allotments seem to be springing up everywhere, and there are those who have even used window boxes that once contained flowers to grow small areas of vegetables. I sometimes wonder how young Bobby would get on if he were to be given a small area of land in order to help the country and grow his own vegetables. He dislikes gardening intensely, but this time it's more a case of necessary duty rather than a hobby. I just hope he remembers to prune my big blackberry bush at the top of the garden. A little care and that will give him some lovely fruit.

God certainly knows what hardships like this can mean. Even famines are mentioned on several occasions in the Scriptures. The prophet Elijah had to deal with a scarcity of food and water when God punished Israel once again for being unfaithful and turning to false gods. However, because God knew that Elijah was faithful to Him, He ordered Elijah to "Leave here, turn eastward and hide in the Kerith Ravine. You will drink from the brook, and I have ordered the ravens to feed you there." So he did what the Lord had told him. He went to the Kerith Ravine, east of the Jordan, and stayed there. 'The ravens brought him bread and meat in the morning and bread and meat in the evening, and he drank from the brook' (1 Kings 17:3-6). When the Israelites escaped from Egypt into the desert, God promised them food in the way of quail and manna, both of which the Israelites had to go out and collect when the time was right. I'm sure that God will make provision for us through other sources but, like the Israelites, let's be ready to collect the food that is there for us.

9

NORWAY AND DENMARK INVADED

Tuesday 30th April 1940

Regardless of Norway's claim to neutrality, Hitler has launched a surprise attack on Norway and Denmark. Denmark has already surrendered, but King Haakon of Norway has promised to "save the freedom of our beloved country". Even so, there are already Nazi sympathisers, led by a Norwegian called Quisling, at work in the country. If Hitler gets into power it will be just like all the Pharisees after the Roman occupation of Israel. The Jewish priests and elders were allowed to carry on with what seemed to be their regular religious duties, as well as having the freedom to make themselves a little better off.

Even I've had personal experience of that. Before the war my father and I had a small bicycle shop. When the war started he found that our bicycle repair services became more profitable, possibly because of the petrol rationing that had been enforced. Many bicycles were just being brought out of the dust that they had gathered in garden sheds or other outhouses on people's property. There were even those who expected repairs for nothing. But people can be like that with money.

As for the Pharisees in old Jerusalem, if they accused anyone of carrying out any form of what they saw as serious anti-religious activity, the final judgement had to be made by the Roman governor in the area. That's exactly what happened to Jesus. The Roman governor, Pontius Pilate, could find no fault in him, but under pressure from the people he agreed that Jesus should be crucified in place of a known thief, Barabbas (Matt. 27:11-26).

10
THE LOW COUNTRIES INVADED

Friday 31st May 1940

On 10th May the German forces surprised us by making a sudden attack into Belgium and Holland, and they are moving quickly into France in what Hitler's generals call a 'Blitzkrieg' (lightning war). We heard the terrifying scream of the dive-bombers as they came in over us first in order to eliminate the main defensive areas. Soon we heard tanks and other armoured vehicles, all of which had infantry support advancing into the woods. The French had built the Maginot Line, a line of fortresses designed to stop any invasion. Unfortunately, the Germans did the unexpected and just went round them. It was obvious that we couldn't hold them for long, and the CO soon received orders to retreat and regroup. As they pushed us further and further back towards the Channel we could all see that desperate measures were needed, and some of the wounded offered to stay behind with heavy machine guns. I left it to the company commander to make the decision, because I felt my sensitive side was saying that it would be committing them to death, however glorious. Fortunately our CO thought the same, and when the enemy advance stopped for the night we managed to slip quietly away toward the field hospital. It took much longer than we anticipated, but the Germans must have been awaiting supplies, which gave us that little extra time to get away to safety.

As Christians we read about Satan and his forces trying to turn us from our Christian beliefs and practices. The trouble is that Satan knows our human weaknesses and may just try something quick and simple in a way we do not expect. As we put our trust in God let's expect the unexpected and be prepared to face it when it comes.

Meanwhile my father has told me that a new group has been formed. This is called the LDV, which stands for Local Defence Volunteers. It is made up of men who are either outside the age limit for regular army troops or perhaps would not be accepted for reasons such as health problems.

This has proved ideal for some of the veterans of the Great War, who still have plenty of fight left in them, though I'm told that as yet there are few weapons to spare. Some of the farmers in the area have got their own shotguns, but the everyday person in the street has to use his imagination and create any weapon they can. Some of them look a bit ragged because they haven't received any official uniforms yet, and their weapons look like something out of history.

11
OPERATION DYNAMO

Sunday 30th June 1940

Well, by the grace of God most of our unit made it back to the Dunkirk beaches. We all felt pretty ragged, and the constant air attacks against the men on the beaches looked like something out of hell. Many were asking which side I thought God was on.

The news headlines on 3rd June were all about the evacuation of nearly 335,000 British and French troops from the beaches of Dunkirk. Winston Churchill's original hopes had been much less than this, but we still lost all our main guns and transport vehicles. They were either left destroyed on the beaches or on the roads leading to the coast in an attempt to obstruct the enemy advance. However, many small ships of every size were called upon either to help ferry troops to the awaiting destroyers or even bring troops back themselves. We all needed a lot of support when we got back from France, so the NAAFI made sure that the town catering van went down to meet the ships when they came in. The soldiers who returned were certainly grateful for a cup of tea. I just feel sorry for some of the guys who were left on the defence perimeters to delay the enemy advance. They did an amazing job, but many had to surrender afterwards. It may not be a victory, but at least we can now regroup our forces at home.

Even so, in much the same way, I don't think God wants us to hide away in our shell once we have accepted the Lord Jesus Christ as our personal Saviour. He may give us duties to perform at any time, so let's make sure we are recharged, maybe through our prayer and reading of the Bible, and through the Holy Spirit - just like a dynamo!

12

FRANCE FALLS

Wednesday 31st July 1940

It's now over two weeks since the French surrender and because I had made friends over there, I was quite upset about their surrender. I had even learned to speak French during my time over there before the war and made several visits to Paris and the surrounding areas. Though the French government claimed that it was due to the lack of British fighter support, there must have been other reasons as well. I wonder if the French were just too reliant on the Maginot Line, and whether they even expected this new type of warfare or whether they were still considering out-of-date Great War tactics. I watched newsreels of Frenchmen in tears as the German soldiers marched through Paris. Hitler has even made a trip to the French capital to gloat over his victory.

We are only human, and expressions of sorrow, together with all our other feelings, are part of human nature. God understands this. The shortest verse in the Bible tells us that even 'Jesus wept' (John 11:35). He saw the sorrow of those around him.

13
THE BATTLE OF BRITAIN STARTS

Saturday 31st August 1940

This has been quite a drastic month. Since the middle of August we have seen swarms of German bombers coming over the coast to bomb targets in the south-east of England.

Initially they tried to knock out our radar stations, which they did with some success, but we have been able to turn to the new Observer Corps to report on the movement of enemy planes. Later on they turned to the main fighter airfields, in the hope of destroying our planes on the ground.

Everyone is concerned about the threat of invasion in the near future, and the Home Guard are busy putting up road blocks and other defences, like disguised pillboxes, in areas both on the beaches and inland. Civil Defence groups are also putting out warnings to beware of spies. Ella Jones runs Wilton Hall, the local bed and breakfast inn. A few weeks ago she had a stranger book in for a few days. His ID papers seemed in order so there didn't seem to be any problem. However, she became suspicious when their guest accidentally used certain speech terms that would only have been used by a foreigner. For example, when asked politely where he had been during the air raid, he replied "I go to shelter." He seemed to be unaware of the use of a past tense in the English language. Ella mentioned this to the authorities, who turned up suddenly on a Wednesday evening. They found the man sitting quietly in his upstairs room listening to a radio - and it certainly wasn't the Home Service he was listening to! I was told that any Germans coming over here trying to speak English like Englishmen need a lot more practice.

Meanwhile, I hear that the Germans have five times as many aircraft as us, but Hitler knows he has to gain air supremacy over the Channel before he can invade. I'm sure our RAF fighter boys will do the best they can to stop him. Not only that, if an enemy aircraft is shot down inland, and survivors are seen to bale out, all the girls try to get there first so they can claim a part of the parachute to make clothes. I'm probably one of those typical males with little or no idea of fashion, so I'm still not sure how they manage to make a reasonably-sized dress from parachute silk.

Our church can have a basic structure, but in our everyday lives we need a way to help us grow stronger in the Lord. Going to church once a week may sometimes not be enough. This is where Home Groups are beneficial. We can meet with other Christians to study and discuss God's Word, and even share our needs in a quieter way with those we know in the group, so becoming stronger in Him.

14

LOOK FOR THE ESCORT!

Monday 30th September 1940

We seem to be winning the air war, and we are still receiving numerous supplies from America, which are sent over in convoys. Without escort ships to defend them they would be easy prey for the U-boats, yet at present there are few warships which can be spared. As the ships leave harbour on their return voyage the captains are told to take their place in the convoy and watch out for any escort ships that will be joining them.

A few years ago my close friend George, who lived in a

nearby village, was a keen yachtsman, and sometimes spent weekends sailing in the coastal areas of Wales. He had already completed a couple of long trips, but the one he had planned was to be the longest of all. This was to be an unescorted trip of about 600 miles to the northern coast of Spain. We watched him leave early one June morning, but we later found that he had forgotten to give his proposed course to any of the coastal authorities. The trip was due to take two weeks, but six months later we were still waiting for news. He had been seen by one of the Cornish lighthouses heading south-east into the Channel some three days after he left, but that was the last time he was seen. In the end he was presumed lost at sea somewhere in the English Channel. His elder son Richard had to take up the reins, so to speak, and when war broke out he joined the RAF. The last I heard was that he was now an ace fighter pilot.

One day when the disciples were on board their own ship, a storm blew up in the sea of Galilee (Luke 8:22-25). Jesus wasn't with them at the time and they feared for their lives, since their small fishing vessel was being tossed about by the wind and waves. However, Jesus miraculously appeared a short distance away, apparently walking on the water, and quelled the storm. Perhaps we have storms in our lives, but Jesus is always there for us. The disciple Peter wanted to walk on the water too, and Jesus called him to come, but as soon as Peter took his eyes off the Lord he started to sink, so arousing his natural sense of fear. Let us, as God's children, always keep our eyes fixed on Jesus.

15
THE UNSEEN NIGHT ENEMY

Thursday 31st October 1940

Since the beginning of the month over 100 German bombers have been coming over every night to attack London. Some of our pilots have been transferred to a night-fighting role, which they find so different, because much of the time you can't even see the attackers during the night. Our fighters must rely heavily on our direction-finding systems to vector them toward their targets, but they still have to rely on their own expertise to see the attackers. There has even been one amusing story of a pilot who claimed to see better in the dark because he ate so many carrots!

Even so, when the dawn comes, one can see the thick smoke hanging over the city and some of the surrounding areas as well. This is because some of the enemy bombers cannot find specific targets, so they simply drop their bombs at random.

However it's not what Jack's son called bad luck. One morning he was taken to his school, only to find that it had been hit by stray bombs. He didn't really like his teacher anyway, so he was quite pleased to be taken back home and told that a replacement school would have to be found for him. He cautiously remarked that it would be okay, so long as they had a different teacher!

Satan can be an unseen enemy too. He can come out of nowhere to strike at our hearts, just as the bombers do to the heart of our country. I thought of the Scripture that tells us "Be self-controlled and alert. Your enemy the devil prowls around like a roaring lion, looking for someone to devour. Resist him, standing firm in the faith, because you know that your brothers throughout the world are undergoing the same kind of suffering" (1 Peter 5:8-9). Let's take every precaution to make sure we are ready.

16
ENEMY ALLIANCES

Saturday 30th November 1940

Political sources have now confirmed that several other countries, including Hungary and Rumania, have signed military alliances with Germany and Italy. I wonder if they considered what might happen to them if Germany loses the war! In our town Julie tells me that there are very few who doubt that we will eventually win the war. Everything's become stalemated at the moment, especially since the Battle of Britain. It proved that we could beat the Germans in the air, so there's no reason to think that once we start building up our forces again, together with all the munitions and other supplies that they require, we can't beat them on land as well.

After the Roman Empire took control of Israel there were many who collaborated with the Romans, including some of the Pharisees, who didn't want to lose their high status. We even read that many of the disciples who followed Jesus to start with simply turned away. But God is mightier than all worldly powers, and in the Book of Revelation it says "The dwelling of God is with men, and he lives with them. They will be his people, and God himself will be with them and be their God. He will wipe every tear from their eyes. There will be no more death or mourning or crying or pain, for the old order of things has passed away" (Rev. 21:3 & 4). He will bring us through safely.

17

FIRE FROM THE SKY!

Tuesday 31st December 1940

It is reported that the Luftwaffe made heavy attacks on the city of London, and the incendiary bombs they dropped caused damage in many areas. The fires could be seen from some distance away, but it could have been even worse, had it not been for the courage of the Civil Defence units, particularly the London Fire Brigade and Ambulance Service, who carried on dousing the flames and rescuing the injured, even though there were times when water supplies were running low.

There's so much to be done everywhere, and so few to do it. Because she lived in North London and knows the area well, Julie has taken on jobs here and there to try and help. She's very good with children, so she helps to look after any who have been left after the mass evacuation of children into the country to escape the bombing. There are even a few young orphans who need special care to try and help them get over the shock of everything. She is able to convince children who have lost one or both parents that they are still loved, and that they still have a place of their own in this world.

There are several references to the fire of the Holy Spirit in the Scriptures. Sometimes the fires that we are seeing in London make people think God's judgement has come upon them. But we believe that though we have to make a big effort, the fire that God is likely to bring down upon those who do not believe in him will be beyond all description.

1941

18

AID AT HAND

Friday 31st January 1941

Senior US diplomat Harry Hopkins has arrived in Britain on a mission from US President Franklin D. Roosevelt to discuss how the USA can help Britain. Though officially the USA wants to remain neutral, it can provide much to keep this country going. However much it is, I hope they get a move on!

At home we are still not sure if or when Hitler might try to invade, or if he's just given up since we won the Battle of Britain. My local pub landlord has become a member of the Home Guard, and he always seems to be busy with the duties associated with that role, and also trying to find enough beer to serve all his customers at the pub. I'm sure he must be getting whatever he can from wherever he can. He may even be brewing some of the beer himself, because I'm told it's very strong! Because our outfit is still refitting, some of the lads go down to the pub regularly, so they can certainly vouch for the beer.

Even so, our current situation reminds me of the time when Jesus said to his disciples "Do not work for food that will spoil, but for food that endures to eternal life, which the Son of Man will give you. On him God the Father has placed his seal of approval" (John 6:27). As we keep looking to God, so he will guide us.

19
AN UNUSUAL RATION

Friday 28th February 1941

In December we heard an unusual report saying that Italy had begun rationing of pasta! News like that certainly tends to arouse one's sense of humour, particularly when everyone round the country has been on strict rationing for some time. If the Italians are expecting Mussolini to provide manna for them I think they are mistaken, particularly after our recent attacks in North Africa where we took many Italian prisoners. Unlike the Germans, the Italian prisoners in the desert were most surprised at our attitude towards them. Some of them were devout Catholics, and we simply reminded them that we were only acting according to God's Word that says "If your enemy is hungry, feed him; if he is thirsty, give him something to drink. In doing this, you will heap burning coals on his head". (Romans 12:20)

The post this month has been late again because of supply problems and the bad weather back home, but I did receive a small package from my mother-in-law Pearl this week which contained a couple of small cakes. I thought it was kind of her and decided to share them with some of the soldiers based here. I'm not sure now whether it was the best thing to do, because the cakes not only had a definite taste of carrot, but I'm almost sure she must have gone to the carpenter's for a touch of spare sawdust for the filling! She may have meant well, but either we are short of some foods at home or Pearl needs a little bit of extra cooking tuition! She said in her letter that father-in-law Frank hates peeling the potatoes for lunch. I think he would probably die laughing if he saw how many more potatoes are peeled and mashed in our cookhouse! I think it was the Duke of Wellington who once said that an army marches on its stomach, so I have to admire all the lads who have orders to do the job. To some it becomes no more than an undesirable, if necessary, repetitive habit, to others a punishment!

20
THE ENEMY
HEROES RETURN

Monday 31st March 1941

The German pocket battleships *Scharnhorst* and *Gneisenau* have returned to port after sinking at least 20 of our merchant ships in the Atlantic. Their sailors returned as heroes, and some were decorated by Hitler himself. He must be gloating over his victories. When I was young I often dreamed of being a hero, but it was as if the opportunity never arose. I think that the closest I've ever been to becoming a hero is through my activities as a lawn bowls umpire. I started this some six years ago, and appear to have an excellent reputation because of my honesty and fairness at all times.

Back in April 1939, just before the war started, I found myself as the only registered umpire in my home county. One other umpire had retired due to ill health and another had moved away. Because of this I was unexpectedly invited along to the annual county players' dinner as a guest. When I went along to see the secretary of the county bowls association to accept the invitation I told him that I felt it was a privilege to be invited, but he laughed out loud. "Well, you're OUR umpire. Now you know what it's like to be popular!" he said.

At least we have some comfort in the Scriptures, which say "He who mocks the poor shows contempt for their Maker, whoever gloats over disaster will not go unpunished". (Proverbs 17:5)

21

MORE LOSSES

Wednesday 30th April 1941

First Yugoslavia, then Greece surrendered, and it won't be long before they consider the island of Crete. Greece didn't even want any help from nearby Allied forces. Things aren't looking good in the Mediterranean. One of the places I visited before the war was the island of Corsica. It had some great local industries, like fishing and lace-making, but these will have been heavily affected by circumstances. In the old days there used to be a group called the Maquis, named after an 18th century patriotic group who carried out guerrilla raids against invading forces then, and were prepared to do so again during this war. In fact, the name Maquis has been linked with the patriots of the resistance groups now active in areas of France.

As Christians, there are always times in our lives when we think everything is going against us. But how will we react? Will we succumb to pressure? Even Jesus had to undergo temptation from the Devil himself, but he demonstrated his worthiness by overcoming Satan's temptations through the power of God's Word. We too can be lifted by the Word and the Promises that God has given unto us in the Scriptures.

22

SINK THE BISMARCK!

Saturday 31st May 1941

Germany's latest and largest battleship, the *Bismarck*, was sighted earlier this month trying to make its way through the Denmark Straits to attack our ships in the Atlantic. When she was engaged by the pride of our fleet, the battlecruiser HMS *Hood* and battleship HMS *Prince of Wales*, we suffered quite a blow when, after only three salvos, a shell penetrated the *Hood*'s thin deck armour and entered the magazine. The entire ship blew up, with only three survivors from the entire complement of nearly 1400 men. *Prince of Wales* was also damaged, but the damage our shells inflicted on the *Bismarck* made her change course and head for France. She was later hit by a torpedo from a Fairey Swordfish that had taken off from our carrier, *Ark Royal*, and her steering gear was disabled. She was then spotted by a Catalina flying boat, which reported that she was going round in circles. Though short of fuel, our battleships *King George V* and *Rodney* then caught up with the *Bismarck* and engaged her with other ships until she was eventually sunk by torpedoes from the cruiser *Dorsetshire*.

Alex is a naval officer who lives with his family just down the road from us. When I met him at home on leave he looked absolutely stunned about the loss of the *Hood*. He told me that many sailors had felt the *Hood* to be the pride of the fleet. He even had a sextant that had been given to him by one of the officers on the *Hood*.

Sometimes we as Christians go round in circles, not knowing which way to turn, wondering whether this or that is the right way to turn. Only by looking to God in prayer can we know what is right, for His Spirit is there to guide us.

23
OPERATION BARBAROSSA

Monday 30th June 1941

It is reported that Hitler has invaded Russia, even though the two countries had signed a non-aggression pact back in 1939! His words were apparently "You only have to kick in the door, and the whole rotten structure will come tumbling down". He must think he's another Joshua fighting for the city of Jericho, but there is one big difference.

Even I've seen a few old barns in the country that look as if they might fall down any moment, and some of the timbers one can see are very rotten. So why don't they fall down when one kicks the door in? Simply because they have a good strong frame, sometimes made of tough oak, that has safely weathered the storms over the years. It takes more than a simple kick at the door to bring those down.

Before the battle Joshua "saw a man standing in front of him with a drawn sword in his hand. Joshua went up to him and asked 'Are you for us or for our enemies?' 'Neither,' he replied, 'but as commander of the army of the Lord I have now come.' Then Joshua fell face down to the ground in reverence, and asked him 'What message does my Lord have for his servant?'" (Joshua 5:13-13) Joshua didn't want to go in and fight the battle as the commander, when he recognized that God was in charge and had sent a heavenly commander under whose power victory would be certain.

24
THE BATTLE FOR MALTA CONTINUES

Thursday 31st July 1941

It's now been over 12 months since the Italians declared war and made their first air attacks on the island of Malta in the Mediterranean. At the time we were woefully unprepared to defend an area of such strategic importance. There were few anti-aircraft guns, and the only air defence at the time was four Sea Gladiator biplanes that were found crated up at the harbour in Valletta. The people named three of these Faith*, Hope and Charity, after the three graces, and they certainly served us well.

The governor on the island, Lt. Gen. Sir William Dobbie, is a committed Christian, and has regularly encouraged the people in prayer. He has inspired the people to stand fast in their prayers of faith. Prayer is not just asking God for something we would like to have. The prayers of those who do it merely as a periodical exercise, and for this reason alone, are likely to get less response. Prayer is important because it is the means by which we are able to establish direct contact with the Almighty God, our Heavenly Father. Through this contact our lives are renewed through the vitalizing power that flows through to us by way of His Holy Spirit.

Author's note: The wreckage of Faith, the only surviving Gladiator, was discovered in a Maltese quarry after the war and is currently being restored at the National War Museum of Malta.

25

THE FINAL SOLUTION

Sunday 31st August 1941

Ever since Hitler came to power in Germany the treatment of the Jews has been terrible. Both he and many others close to him have expressed their disgust at them, and steps have been taken to promptly remove or isolate any known Jews. Those who are still alive remain in fear of their lives today, and one of the promises that Hitler made was that he would eliminate the Jews completely. Signs of his anti-Semitic tyranny are already apparent in the countries that he has invaded and taken control of, where many Jews are being ousted from their homes, to be 'resettled', it is said. That sounds ominous.

As for being in fear of our lives, I was watching *Arizona Days*, one of the traditional cowboy films starring Tex Ritter that is shown on our base every week. It's nice to think that one could be the cowboy who's quickest on the draw, who has a couple of faithful friends by his side, and who is admired by all the girls looking for a husband. If he were the town sheriff I wouldn't want to be an outlaw wanting to come in on horseback and rob the bank.

There are many times in the Scriptures when we read of the Israelites being at war with other nations in the Middle East. There were wars against the Assyrians, the Babylonians, the Philistines and other kingdoms and tribes. Yet they didn't always win. There were times when God allowed punishment to come upon His people because of their idolatry or wickedness. In 587 BC the city of Jerusalem was plundered and burned by the Babylonian king Nebuchadnezzar, and the Israelites were sent into exile, but God promised then, as now, "I will take the Israelites out of the nations where they have gone. I will gather them from all around and bring them back into their own land" (Ezekiel 37:21). He also promises "My dwelling-place will be with them. I will be their God, and they will be my people" (Ezekiel 37:27). Our God is a faithful God who always keeps His promises.

26
A TOUCHING MOMENT

Tuesday 30th September 1941

Well, it's now been two years since war was declared, and we haven't given in, as Hitler thought we would. I've been on leave this week, so I thought I would visit a few friends at home. I had quite a surprise when even my old bank manager turned up in an air raid warden's uniform! There has been a lot of bombing in the nearby areas, but I think that's easing off now, and we seem to be giving it back even more. One mate had a lucky escape after he and a couple of others met for an evening together. Just as an air raid started, he remembered that he had a message to deliver to a lady in the nearby street, so he left the house for a moment. When he got there he found nothing but rubble. The house had received a direct hit, and the family inside were trapped underneath it all. The Civil Defence managed to get the man out safely, but his wife had been on the ground floor, and the complete weight of the house must have come down upon her. She had no chance.

As Christians we sometimes have to endure real moments of hardship, and maybe make sacrifices. Abraham had to do the same. God had kept His promise to Abraham by giving him a son but, as perhaps what one would call a part of the bargain, He wanted to see if Abraham's faith in Him really was complete. For this reason, God gave him perhaps one of the hardest tasks imaginable. He was to take his only son Isaac and offer him as a sacrifice. Only at the last moment did God stay Abraham's hand, for He could see that Abraham had done everything that God asked in simple obedience. Because of his obedience Abraham was greatly blessed, and the angel of the Lord spoke to him a second time, saying "I swear by myself, says the Lord, that because you have done this and have not withheld your son, your only son, I will surely bless you and make your descendants as numerous as the stars in the sky and as the sand on the seashore. Your descendants will take possession of the cities of their enemies, and through your offspring all nations on earth will be blessed, because you have obeyed me." (Genesis 22:15-17)

27

MOSCOW UNDER THREAT

Friday 31st October 1941

So far the German forces have made great headway, and their advance continues, even though there have been counterattacks by the Russian forces. It looks as if they are heading for Moscow. The Russian dictator, Josef Stalin, appears to have roused all the forces in the city. Many of the civilian population are being used to dig large anti-tank defences around the city, whilst others are busy preparing other lines of defence.

There are times when we feel weak, and would certainly not consider ourselves fit to lead an army. Yet here again, God uses us to perform tasks not in our strength, but in His. In the early days in the Promised Land there were wars with different tribes. In the Book of Judges we are told of Gideon, who thought little of himself. God spoke to him during the war against the Midianites and said "Go in the strength you have and save Israel out of Midian's hand. Am

I not sending you?" Gideon was puzzled, and replied "But Lord, how can I save Israel? My clan is the weakest in Manasseh, and I am the least in my family." However, God already knew this, and replied "I will be with you, and you will strike down the Midianites together" (Judges 6:14-16). This gave Gideon the reassurance that he needed.

I've just been watching one of the Charlie Chaplin films. They are so funny, especially when you see him almost waddling down the road with his cane stick and bowler hat. He often makes a mess of things, but then he is the hero, and things tend to get put right. He's another one who could be described as a bit of a weakling.

28
JAPANESE OPEN NEGOTIATIONS WITH USA

Sunday 30th November 1941

The Japanese invaded China and other far eastern territories by force through the 1930s, and the struggle there continues. The main excuse is that they seriously required the resources that these areas could provide. Last July the USA was said to have frozen all Japanese assets, but negotiations have opened in Washington between the two countries. The USA has demanded a complete Japanese withdrawal from China and French Indo-China. The new Japanese Prime Minister, Hidekei Tojo, has maintained a warlike attitude, and many are concerned about what it might lead to if negotiations break down.

There's an area of the town that's been specially put by for some of the Chinese refugees that have been drifting in. A number of them have been used as labourers, though some of them can hardly speak a word of English. Yet whatever job they have been given, the Chinese always seem willing and very busy. I suppose that's a reflection of what life has been like in China, though I'm sure many of them came over here to stay alive, rather than face a patriotic death that would be seen of little consequence.

Before the oppressed Israelites left Egypt on their long Exodus to the Promised Land, Moses had words with the Egyptian Pharaoh and asked him to release the people. Pharaoh stood his ground. The 10 plagues were brought upon Egypt and, after each one, the stubborn Pharaoh temporarily relented, only to change his mind once again (Exodus 7-11). He only let them go after the plague of the firstborn (Exodus 11), when his eldest son died. Even after that, when the Israelites were on their way out of Egypt, he changed his mind again and pursued them with his chariots, all of which were lost in the Red Sea. I wonder how he felt after that.

29
PEARL HARBOR ATTACKED!

Wednesday 31st December 1941

There has been a sudden attack on the American Pacific Fleet at the port of Pearl Harbor in Hawaii by Japanese carrier-based air forces. President Franklin D. Roosevelt stated: "Yesterday, December 7th, 1941 - a date which will live in infamy - the United States of America was suddenly and deliberately attacked by naval and air forces of the Empire of Japan. The United States was at peace with that nation, and, at the solicitation of Japan, was still in conversation with its government and its Emperor looking toward the maintenance of peace in the Pacific." Before asking Congress to make an official declaration of war, he added "With confidence in our armed forces, with the unbounding determination of our people, we will gain the inevitable triumph. So help us God." On 10th December Hitler decided to declare war on America as well, so we're all in the same boat now.

I would like to think that the President's speech sets an example for all of us in this war. Over in England we have certainly had to face hardships, but the determination that it aroused can be seen everywhere. We're certainly not going to buckle at the knees, but we will certainly have to show patience before this war is won.

Meanwhile, how determined are we to follow in the path that God has set for us? The task He has given us to perform may not be easy, but will we turn aside or follow in the path that God has prepared for us.

1942

30
THE SIEGE OF LENINGRAD CONTINUES

Saturday 31st January 1942

Hitler's Army Group North moved up to attack Leningrad, one of Russia's most important industrial centres, some three months ago. At first things looked dire, because almost all communication facilities were lost, and with the Red Army having suffered the loss of hundreds of thousands of men either killed or taken prisoner, there seemed little hope of resupply. However, probably because Hitler wanted to use as many forces as he had available at the time to attack Moscow, he decided not to attack Leningrad directly but lay siege to the city to force the people into starvation. Every day the enemy artillery batteries bombard the city with shells. Unfortunately, many people have died of hunger, and there are reports that hundreds, if not thousands, of the population are dying of starvation each day. However, there is a slim chance that the frozen Lake Ladoga, to the north-west of the city, may be used as an iced road to help bring in some supplies, together with reinforcements.

I wonder if they are using any sledges over there. Julie tells me that our grocer has being going round delivering food on a sledge, because he's had to deal with petrol rationing himself, and it's certainly been cold enough to use a sledge on some of the roads. I expect Bobby will have got his sledge out of the garden shed as well, because there are a few slopes round town that he could use it on.

How often did God supply food to the hungry? He's certainly helped us out at home, because more American supplies seem to be getting through across the Atlantic. There are the well-known events like the feeding of the children of Israel during their 40 years in the desert. We also know that Jesus fed crowds of over 4,000 and 5,000. But often we find that the food referred to in Jesus' ministry is spiritual food. He spoke of the manna given to the Israelites in the desert and stressed that it was God who fed them, and gave them the true bread from heaven. Jesus then referred to Himself when He added "For the bread of God is he who comes down from heaven and gives life to the world." (John 6:33) The disciples did not quite understand, but must have realised that the bread that Jesus spoke of was special, and were eager to be provided with it. Jesus responded "I am the bread of life. He who comes to me will never go hungry, and he who believes in me will never be thirsty" (John 6:35)

31
FALL OF SINGAPORE

Saturday 28th February 1942

The Japanese invaded Malaya at the same time as the

attack on Pearl Harbor and have made great advances. Even the British fortress of Singapore, once thought to be impregnable, has now surrendered, with thousands taken prisoner. The total number could be around 130,000. Yet it was revealed that the Japanese army had only numbered about 35,000 soldiers. General Percival, the commander of the forces in Singapore, may have overestimated the number of Japanese troops attacking. All our main guns were pointing seaward, and this is no doubt one of the main reasons why the Japanese invaded Singapore from the landward side, something for which we had not prepared.

To have succumbed to such a small force is incredible, but it isn't the first time that something like this has happened. In the struggle against the Midianites, God told Gideon that he had "too many men for me to deliver Midian into their hands" (Judges 7:2a). The reason given was that the Israelites "should not boast against me that her own strength has saved her" (Judges 7:2b). By a process of selection the Israelite army was reduced from 32,000 men to only 300, to which Gideon gave strict instructions as to strategy. When they came to Gideon after the battle, they said "Rule over us - you, your son, and your grandson - because you have saved us out of the hand of Midian." But Gideon remembered that it was only because of what God had done that the victory had been gained, so he replied "I will not rule over you, nor will my son rule over you. The Lord will rule over you" (Judges 8:22-23). Gideon worshipped God for His strength, rather than let Israel boast in the human victory that had been won.

Well, I may not have any grandsons yet, but if or when we do I wonder if young Bobby will see me as a Gideon? I'm sure that he'd rather, and quite rightly, take charge of his own family. When I got married my in-laws were all very nice about things, but I've always felt that they would like to retain a bit of power over me and Julie.

32
NEW HEAVY BOMBER INTRODUCED

Tuesday 31st March 1942

One of the pilots on the nearby RAF base was showing me a model aircraft that he had cut out of some old wooden blocks. He told me his son wanted a Spitfire, so he's done the best he can, with a little help from his mates, to make a scale model. It certainly looks quite impressive. He's a bomber pilot, but finding all the bits and bobs to make up a model bomber would have been quite a difficult task.

Up to now we have been relying very much on our medium bombers, especially the twin-engined Vickers Wellington, for which the geodetic basket-weave fuselage construction, designed by Barnes Wallis, helped to provide a strong yet lightweight structure. However, at present, even though the Germans have to take shelter when we make a raid into Germany itself, the time spent in the shelters cannot be very long, because both the bomb load and range of the Wellingtons are rather less than required.

With more raids into Germany planned, we have been looking for a new design of heavy bomber. We already have the Short Stirling and the Handley-Page Halifax available, both of which went into production last year, but one aircraft in particular seems to have gained the approval of all the pilots who tested it. This is the twin-tailed, four-engined Avro Lancaster, which has now entered service with the RAF. It was developed from the less successful Avro Manchester, which had three rudders but was underpowered with only two engines. The Avro Lancaster is powered by four Rolls Royce Merlin engines, which are the same type as those fitted in our Spitfire and Hurricane fighters. This gives it a range of over 2,000 miles with a bomb load of nearly 22,000 pounds, as well as having good defensive armament. It has also proved itself to be the fastest of our heavy bombers, and is very manoeuvrable. The Lancs that we have seen recently out on mine-laying duties are a real treat to watch, and it's heavy bombers like this with a longer range and a greater bomb load that we need to take the war to the enemy.

When we first started we only had a few vulnerable light or medium bombers, and it was like standing with our slings facing an Old Testament army armed with chariots and swords. But then we all know what happened to the Philistine Goliath!

33

THE DOOLITTLE RAID

Thursday 30th April 1942

Due to a lack of intelligence reports, the Japanese, when they raided Pearl Harbor last December, found that none of the American aircraft carriers, which were considered important targets, were in port. Even so, Japan considered itself too far away from any Allied airfields to be attacked from the air. For this reason they did little to develop their anti-aircraft defences. This has now been proved costly, because several flights of B-25 medium bombers, led by Lieutenant Colonel James H. Doolittle, have carried out raids on Tokyo and other targets in the Japanese home islands. The bombers had been stripped of all excess weight to enable them to take off successfully from the aircraft carrier *Hornet*. The raid caused little overall damage, but took the Japanese completely by surprise and rather dented their impression that they were impregnable. It also boosted the morale of the American people, who had been the victims of the unprovoked attack on Pearl Harbor. It was too far for the B-25s to fly back to the carrier, so it was intended that the surviving aircraft head for friendly territory in China. Each plane had directions to their individual targets, and the pilots had to be very receptive to the information provided by the on-board navigator.

This week everything has been absolutely hectic, and no peace at all. Everyone seems in a rush, and it's been almost impossible to start any conversations. No one seems to want to listen to anyone else. I suppose everyone would rather wait for some good news than gossiping on about everything that's gone wrong so far. I can't really blame them! Meanwhile, after all this time back in England retraining there's a strong feeling around the base that we'll soon be back on active duty again. There are issues of tropical kit arriving at the quartermaster's hut, but we still don't know where we might be posted.

When we want to hear from God, we need to be receptive as well. When Jacob was going through a bad time, God spoke to him in a dream, saying "I am with you, and will watch over you wherever you go" (Genesis 28:15). When he woke the next morning, even Jacob admitted that "Surely the Lord is in this place, and I was not aware of it." (v.16) The same happened to young Samuel when God spoke to him in the temple. At first he thought it was the priest Eli calling him, but Eli eventually realised it was the Lord, and told Samuel that when it happened again, he should answer "Speak, Lord, for your servant is listening" (1 Samuel 3). So how receptive are we to God today? He may be there waiting to speak, but are we ready to listen?

34

OPERATION MILLENNIUM

Sunday 31st May 1942

The first 1,000 bomber raid, aptly called Operation Millennium, has been carried out against the German city of Cologne, causing tremendous fire damage throughout the city. When he took charge of Bomber Command in the spring, Air Chief Marshal Sir Arthur Harris, known to all as 'Bomber' Harris, made a broadcast to the country about his widespread 'carpet bombing' tactics. During the news broadcast Harris laid the reasons for his bombing plan squarely on the shoulders of the German air force, which had caused so much damage to British cities. But it was strange that he then quoted a verse from the Old Testament prophet Hosea, saying "They have sowed the wind, and now they will reap the whirlwind" (Hosea 8:7). He seems to think that he can win this war all on his own by all this bombing, but I'm not the only one to have doubts about his tactics. The bombing itself can certainly do a lot of damage, but that doesn't necessarily mean that it will destroy the people's will to fight. He should remember that from when London got bombed so heavily.

Much of the book of Hosea deals with the children of Israel, many of whom had turned away from God, and were following in the ways of wickedness with an unrepentant heart. God really had no choice but to punish them for lives that had become so unfaithful to Him. But His love for the children of Israel does not stop. He implores them to be wise and return to Him. The Scriptures read "Who is wise? He will realise these things. Who is discerning? He will understand them. The ways of the Lord are right, the righteous walk in them, but the rebellious stumble in them" (Hosea 14:9). We have the choice - to follow in the way of the Lord or not!

Our posting came through early this month, and whoever put their money on Africa was right. After several days suffering the stench, seasickness and other discomforts of sitting in a grimy cramped hold of a small troop transport we eventually landed in Egypt. Now we've got sand under our feet and in the air. We've even nicknamed our cook Sandy because much of the food from his small outdoor kitchen seems to be served with sand in it.

35
THE BATTLE OF MIDWAY

Tuesday 30th June 1942

The Americans have won a great victory at the battle of Midway in the Pacific. Japanese forces, led by Admiral Nagumo, the same admiral who led their forces into the attack on Pearl Harbor, recognised that Midway was the gateway for their bombing raids on the west coast of America. They first sent a diversionary force to attack the Aleutians to the north. It was also hoped that if the Americans took forces to counter this invasion, then the fleet might include the aircraft carriers which the Japanese had missed at Pearl Harbor. They attacked the island from the air in order to neutralise the defences before the invasion force landed. They had not expected much resistance, but the old Brewster Buffalo fighters on the island put up a stiff, if suicidal, battle.

It is rumoured that American Intelligence knew about the raid and had sent three aircraft carriers under the command of Admiral Spruance to intercept the Japanese fleet once they attacked. This they did with great success over the next three days, destroying four Japanese fleet carriers and two cruisers for the loss of a single aircraft carrier, the *USS Yorktown*. Had Midway been occupied, then the whole west coast of America would have been under threat from enemy ships and aircraft based there.

I wonder if they would have thought the same as us when we started to face the enemy bombing raids? I'm not even sure if they even have a blackout yet, and the newer American recruits that have been sent over here have made it clear that they want their families to carry on with a near normal life. They've added that many are going into the industrial production centres to try and find jobs producing wartime essentials like ammunition, planes, tanks and ships.

After the crossing of the Red Sea and the destruction of the following Egyptian army, Moses wrote his own words of worship. They include "The enemy boasted, 'I will pursue, I will overtake them. I will divide the spoils, I will gorge myself on them. I will draw my sword and my hand will destroy them.' But you blew with your breath, and the sea covered them. They sank like lead in the mighty waters. Who among the gods is like you, O Lord? Who is like you - majestic in holiness, awesome in glory, working wonders?" (Exodus 15:9-11)

36
ARCTIC CONVOY PQ17
ATTACKED

Friday 31st July 1942

One of our recent convoys en route to Murmansk with supplies for the Russians has suffered heavy losses. The Arctic convoy was made up of 33 merchant ships and a tanker, together with numerous escort vessels. We understand that about 20 of these ships have been lost to aircraft and enemy submarines. A warning was sent, but it is said that because Sir Dudley Pound, the First Lord of the Admiralty, had received incorrect information that the enemy battleship *Tirpitz* was also under way to attack the convoy, the decision was made to scatter the convoy earlier than necessary. Because the convoy became so scattered, enemy forces lost no time intercepting any stragglers or single ships they could find.

It all made me think of our local football team, when they get scattered around on the field of play. There might be a fullback trying to clear the ball, and if the players aren't in their right positions then the ball could well be intercepted by one of the opposing team.

We too have times as Christians when our fears or doubts make us want to scatter. But in doing so we leave ourselves even more open to temptation and sin. The apostle Paul wrote "The body is a unit, though it is made up of many parts; and though all its parts are many, they form one body. So it is with Christ. For we were all baptised by one Spirit into one body - whether Jews or Greeks, slave or free - and we were all given the one Spirit to drink" (1 Corinthians 12:12-13). Throughout this chapter of the Bible, Paul says that every part of the body, whether weak or strong, has its own task to perform. As we have fellowship with other Christians, so we can be strengthened or given support in what we do.

37
OPERATION PEDESTAL

Monday 31st August 1942

A big operation, named Pedestal, has been carried out in a major attempt to resupply Malta. There were already suggestions that the island, because of all the enemy air attacks, which caused severe starvation and destroyed fuel and ammunition stocks, could not have survived for more than a couple more weeks. However, five of the merchantmen that set out from Gibraltar have now arrived in Grand Harbour, Valetta, to a tumultuous welcome from the crowds. One of the ships that arrived safely, though badly damaged, was the tanker *Ohio*, which entered the harbour proudly lashed to the two destroyers HMS *Bramham* and HMS *Penn*. The Maltese called this the Santa Marija Convoy, since it was due to arrive on 13th August, the Feast of the Virgin Mary, and many prayers had been said around the island. They were greatly encouraged when the first four ships arrived on that day, and even more so when the *Ohio* arrived two days later. They saw it as divine intervention.

God knows all our needs. We may not all be in such a desperate situation but let us, just like the Maltese, demonstrate our faith in God through the prayers we give unto Him, and let us also give Him all the glory for what we receive.

38
USS WASP SUNK NEAR GUADALCANAL

Wednesday 30th September 1942

We haven't had any post for 2 weeks. After routing the

Italians here in North Africa things looked good, but we got pushed back just as quickly when Hitler sent the Afrika Korps to reinforce them. When they counter-attacked their tanks and field guns were just too good for us. It's so hard to accept all the defeats we've had, and everywhere I go I get asked the same question again and again - "Why? Why? Why?" We just can't go on like this! There have to be big changes made in our weapons, our tactics, and also at the top with some of our commanders.

The American aircraft carrier *USS Wasp* has also been torpedoed by a Japanese submarine off the island of Guadalcanal in the Solomons. There were nearly 200 casualties, and one of those was the war correspondent Jack Singer. He was one of the notable International News Service (INS) reporters assigned to cover the war in the Pacific. A war correspondent's job is filled with danger, yet the news that they bring back can be a morale-lifter, and can also be of assistance to intelligence sources. Wherever I am posted, I have to make sure I keep my eyes and ears open, not only to get a view of any enemy threat, but also any possible strategic sites that the enemy might decide to use. Anything like that is also of assistance to intelligence sources.

As the early Christians found, life was hard, but when missionaries travelled afield they brought encouragement to the new churches. Paul found that other apostles gave him reports on the progress of the churches. Some, he found, were getting on well. In his letter to the church at Rome, Paul writes "First, I thank my God for all of you, because your faith is being reported all over the world" (Romans 1:8). Others had more problems. He wrote to the church in Galatia "I am astonished that you are so quickly deserting the one who called you by the grace of Christ and are turning to a different gospel - which is really no gospel at all" (Galatians 1:6-7a).

How do we stand?

39

THE FOX IS ON THE RUN!

Saturday 31st October 1942

Well, there certainly have been changes and, from what we can see, they are very much for the better. At the end of August we held Rommel, commonly known as the 'Desert Fox', back in North Africa. Last month, while he has been regrouping, the commander of the 8th Army, Lieutenant-General Bernard Montgomery, usually known as 'Monty', organised our defensive line near the old railway station of El Alamein. With one end of the line near the coast and another next to the sinking sand of the Qattara Depression, Rommel couldn't outflank us. During the first day of the battle Monty opened fire with around 900 guns, together with around 1000 tanks and infantry in the rear, ready for when the breakthrough came. Later the mine clearance units will go in, backed up by the infantry, to prepare a path for the main assault units. Any stranger round here would have thought that we were having an early bonfire night with plenty of fireworks, including a lot of bangers.

Given the lack of fuel, and with the Afrika Korps in danger of being destroyed where it stood, Rommel may have no option but to withdraw. However, if we get the advantage here, and with the Americans' amphibious landings in Tunisia imminent, Rommel has real problems. He will need to withdraw fast but may find he's got nowhere to go!

I know what's it's like having to withdraw suddenly. When I was at school I was still quite shy, so a couple of the bigger boys tended to bully me out of sight of the teacher. They wanted to fight me, and called me a coward for not doing so, but whatever my heart wanted me to do, my head said that it would be wiser just to stay at a distance. Those boys persisted at me, but in the end they did it once too often and were expelled from the school.

As Christians there is only one way to go, and that is along the path that God has prepared for us, even though we can't always expect it to be easy. It's something we can only do by our faith in Him and our obedience to His Word. Jesus is our way, and He will be our guide. Yet there are those who find it hard to continue in God's way, and wander from it. Perhaps they have doubts, perhaps they are under the impression that their way can be easier, and so cannot make that full commitment to Him. If we seek to go our own way, then we are denying God, and God's warning to us is simple: "For those who are self-seeking, and who reject the truth and follow evil, there will be wrath and anger. There will be trouble and distress for every human being who does evil; first for the Jew, then for the Gentile; but glory, honour, peace for everyone who does good; first for the Jew, then for the Gentile. God does not show favouritism" (Romans 2:8-11).

40
ASSAULT ON
GUADALCANAL CONTINUES

Monday 30th November 1942

Back in August the US Marines landed on the Pacific island of Guadalcanal, where they headed for a Japanese airstrip under construction and nearing completion. The Marines captured the airfield, which they renamed Henderson Field, at heavy cost to both them and the Japanese defenders. Their suicidal attitude, particularly in the Banzai charges where they all mass together and attack head-on like the old assaults in the Great War, is to do with the old Samurai warrior tradition, which insists that surrender would bring dishonour to both a warrior and his family. The Japanese prefer to die in battle or, if there is no hope, to commit suicide.

Counterattacks by Japanese reinforcements during September and October have been held back. The recent naval engagement took place at such close range that the American battleships were unable to lower their guns enough to bring them to bear on the enemy fleet. Even so, a number of Japanese transports and heavy warships were sunk, and it is now believed that it won't be long before the island is secured.

After a long wait we've even had the post flown in to Egypt via Gibraltar. This was a big relief to us all, because things can get very lonely out here. My Julie and little

Bobby are really having to push themselves to the limit now, because they have now had to cut back on heating fuel. Now that winter's here everyone seems to be using more and more wood on their fires, and it's hard to find enough of it. Most of the coal is now being used by the various wartime industries, so very little of it is available for domestic use.

How secure do we feel in our everyday lives as Christians? Do we feel that we are not doing enough to quite make the grade for God's Eternal Life? Be reassured, for the apostle Peter writes "His divine power has given us everything we need for life and godliness through our knowledge of Him who called us by His own glory and goodness. Through these He has given us His very great and precious promises, so that through them you may participate in the divine nature and escape the corruption in the world caused by evil desires" (2 Peter 1:3-4). He adds that as Christians, we should "be all the more eager to make your calling and election sure. For if you do these things, you will never fall, and you will receive a rich welcome into the eternal kingdom of our Lord and Saviour Jesus Christ" (vv. 10-11). Our lives, both earthly and eternal, are secure in Him.

41
DEVELOPMENT OF OBOE

Thursday 31st December 1942

Though the main details are still secret, I have been told by a few close friends in Bomber Command that a new bombing guidance system, commonly known as OBOE, is currently being tested. A small force of De Havilland Mosquitoes used it on a trial target earlier this month, and it was found to be very accurate. Apparently the aircraft fly at a constant range from one Oboe station, whilst the correct instant for bomb release is decided automatically by the controller at a second Oboe station. It has been suggested that the fast Mosquito fighter-bomber should act as a pathfinder, dropping visual markers on the aiming point ready for the main force. Once this has been done then the Mosquito would use its speed to avoid enemy nightfighters and return to its home base.

Not being a very good pilot, as I look outside and see the stars glittering in their God-given places across the sky, I wonder how aircraft could make their way through the night to a particular area in order to drop its bombs. Julie has always told me that my direction finding skills are negative, and that if I were taken along the road to visit a house then I would never get back again! She reminded me of the time when all the signposts were being removed from the roads as a precaution, just in case there was a German invasion, and because of it I ended up deep in the forest. I must write and ask what their Christmas has been like. Bobby loves a share of plum pudding but, like the traditional turkeys, I don't know if there are too many around this year.

Sometimes we need a marker or sign to guide us in our Christian lives. Jesus gave His disciples signs throughout His time of ministry on earth. He carried out miracles of healing, and other spectacular feats like the feeding of the 5,000 (Mark 6:30-44) for all to see. Yet how would we have responded to such signs? Would we dismiss them as a trick of science, or would we truly accept in our hearts that He is the Messiah, the Son of God, and so follow in His way. For Christ Himself said "I am the Way and the Truth and the Life. No-one comes to the Father except through me." (John 14:6)

1943

42
CHANGES IN THE GERMAN HIGH COMMAND

Sunday 31st January 1943

There are reports that Grand Admiral Erich Raeder, who has been the head of the Kriegsmarine, has now resigned and will be replaced by Admiral Dönitz, who has been in charge of the successful enemy U-boat fleet. Though loyal to the Fuehrer, Admiral Raeder did not necessarily agree to all Hitler's policies, and this may well be one of the main reasons for his replacement. I think they take their ideas a lot more seriously over there.

For a long time, during our engagement, my wife Julie and I didn't agree on what life was to be like after we got married. If we had children, she wanted a girl and I wanted a boy. I was lucky in that respect! She wanted a house in a relatively peaceful rural area of the country, whilst I would have been quite happy with a nice-sized flat near to where she already lived. She got her way with that in the end! But through all our plans we had one real purpose in mind. We wanted to be a couple with a child of our own to care for, and seek to have as happy a life as possible together. There has been a little bit of give and take in our married lives, but in doing so we have really achieved what we wanted.

In our Christian life, can God rely on us to carry out

whatever tasks may lie ahead? Though our faith may be strong, no doubt there are times when we think that something is just too much for us. Yet God, who is supreme over all, is still there to help us, for we are His children. It is written "So we say with confidence, 'The Lord is my helper; I will not be afraid. What can man do to me?'" (Hebrews 13:6)

43
VICTORY AT STALINGRAD

Sunday 28th February 1943

We have heard that the entire German 6th Army under the command of recently-promoted Field Marshal von Paulus has surrendered to the Russians at Stalingrad. The Russians took 91,000 prisoners, including 24 German generals! The airlift of supplies that had been promised by Field Marshal Milch of the German air force had failed, and many soldiers were suffering from hunger and the severe cold of the Russian winter, for which they were totally unprepared. For example, Hitler had expected a quick victory and, perhaps a bit like us at the beginning of the war, had made no provision for winter clothing.

As Christians we will face events for which we may be unprepared. In the days following the birth of the Christian

Church in Jerusalem there followed a wave of persecution. King Herod's persecution had already caused the death of Stephen by stoning (Acts 7:54-60), and soon after the disciple James died, then Peter was suddenly imprisoned in a maximum security jail. Here there were four soldiers on guard at all times, two with Peter and two on the door. Yet God saw Peter's need and sent an angel to release him, miraculously releasing Peter's chains and opening the prison door. Only after they had walked the length of one street did the angel disappear and Peter came round, after feeling quite baffled at first. He soon said "Now I know without a doubt that the Lord sent his angel and rescued me from Herod's clutches and from everything the Jewish people were anticipating" (Acts 12:10).

44
ROMMEL RETURNS TO GERMANY

Wednesday 31st March 1943

It has been reported that Field Marshal Erwin Rommel, the commander of the German Afrika Korps, has returned to Germany on sick leave. He disobeyed Hitler directly by retreating back across North Africa following our victory at El Alamein, rather than defending the territory to the last man, as ordered. However, it seems more likely that he has been flown out by Hitler to undertake another command elsewhere.

There comes a time when circumstances catch up with all of us. I had a letter from the Major in command of my local Salvation Army group, sending me his and the group's best wishes and hopes for a safe return, but he added that even he would be due for replacement in the near future. This was a disappointment, because I had known the old Major for some time, and the Salvation Army was his whole life.

Moses, who had led the children of Israel out of Egypt, had also been told by God that because of the disobedience that God had seen amongst the Israelites he would not be allowed to cross into the Promised Land. But God did make one concession, and allowed Moses to view the Promised Land across the Jordan River. His orders were "Look at the land with your own eyes, since you are not going to cross the Jordan. But commission Joshua, and encourage and strengthen him, for he will lead this people across and will cause them to inherit the land that you will see." (Deuteronomy 3:27-28)

45
DEATH OF ADMIRAL YAMAMOTO

Friday 30th April 1943

A few days ago the Japanese fleet broadcast details of a tour of inspection by Admiral Yamamoto, who was Japan's most revered, most intelligent and most determined warlord. He was also considered irreplaceable. It was he who planned the attack on the American fleet at Pearl Harbor. After the partial success of the operation, Yamamoto realised that Japan was not fully prepared for a long war against America and commented that they had woken "a sleeping giant", especially after he heard that Japan's declaration of war had not been delivered until after the attack was under way, something which he knew would arouse the fury of the American people.

We too have feelings. I've often showed anger, as well as understanding and love, especially towards my family and close friends. So had Jesus, who showed anger towards the marketeers in the temple (John 2:12-17), and compassion towards Jairus, whose daughter he raised from the dead. Yet why did Jesus accept his fate on the cross of Calvary so easily? He just knew that God had sent him, and it was his task to die upon the cross bearing the sin of mankind upon him. Through Him we are redeemed!

46
AXIS FORCES SURRENDER
IN NORTH AFRICA

Monday 31st May 1943

On 13th May General Alexander sent a signal to Winston Churchill. It said simply "Sir, it is my duty to report that the Tunisian campaign is over. All enemy resistance has ceased. We are masters of the North African shores." Today, we have been watching the victory parade here in Tunis, with Monty in his staff car, standing to salute the thousands of cheering troops lining the roadside.

It sounds just like the FA Cup Final at Wembley. When I went there in April 1939 I saw a brilliant match between Portsmouth and Wolves, the team I supported, but in the end Portsmouth won 4-1, and after the Cup had been presented to the captain, Jimmy Guthrie, the team came back onto the pitch, where he lifted it high to show their supporters. It was as if he was thinking to himself, "Well, today we are masters of Wembley and the whole of the Football League!"

In his letter to the church at Corinth, Paul speaks of the victory we have already won through the resurrection of the Lord Jesus Christ, and writes "Death is swallowed up in victory" (1 Corinthians 15:54b). He adds "But thanks be to God! He gives us victory through our Lord Jesus Christ.

Therefore, my dear brothers, stand firm. Let nothing move you. Always give yourselves fully to the work of the Lord, because you know that your labour in the Lord is not in vain" (1 Cor. 15:58). As Christians it is our task to follow in His way. In order to gain the victory let us not stray as we seek to undertake what lies ahead.

47
THE RESISTANCE MOVEMENT

Wednesday 30th June 1943

For some time, in a number of the countries that were taken over by the Germans, there has been an organised resistance movement. Not only do we have many agents who have been dropped into enemy territory by parachute, there are still many of the local population who resent the occupation and are prepared to help in whatever way they can. Not only do they try and hinder or sabotage enemy communications or supply depots, they also provide valuable information for the Allies regarding the strength of enemy forces in their area. This is a dangerous task, because not only have a number of those involved been caught and executed, but members of their family as well. The ruthless invaders often use torture first as a means of getting information. I admire their courage, because many French patriots prefer to face death rather than betray friends or give other secrets away.

Even so, resistance is nothing new. At the time of Jesus there was much bitterness toward their Roman invaders. After Pontius Pilate had interviewed Jesus in Jerusalem, he gave the people of Jerusalem the choice of whether to free Jesus or Barabbas, a well-known troublemaker for the Romans. The people chose Barabbas. In some respects the Roman soldiers approved of this. They would rather crucify someone who they saw as King of the Jews than some petty troublemaker. It would demonstrate their authority over the Jews.

48
BATTLE OF KURSK

Saturday 31st July 1943

Our Prime Minister is a little suspicious of the Russians. For two years now we have been supplying them through our Arctic convoys, and our merchant fleet has suffered heavy losses from both aircraft and submarines. It's hard to think of what a sailor's thoughts might be if his ship were to be torpedoed.

Our CO has selected me for a special mission. On 8th

July I was due to be flown back to England, where I would be given a final briefing. It seems a shame that I had to be transferred away, after sharing life - and sometimes death - with the same lads for so long. Still, orders are orders. When I arrived back I was given 24 hours leave, and told where to report afterwards. It gave me the opportunity to visit Julie and Bobby again, and it was a lovely surprise for us all.

Having reported back promptly I was told that I would be acting as a diplomatic aide to a general with a mission in Russia. It looks like we are being sent in as go-betweens to find out what they really need. My Russian may not be good, but it's certainly acceptable for the job in hand.

Stalin doesn't care for underdogs, so I have been given a special, if temporary, high rank. Because of the Russian advances into the Kursk salient south of Moscow, the enemy decided to try attacking with a pincer movement from the northern and southern areas in order to cut their supplies off. It appears a big tank battle has been taking place, but the Russians are confident that their new mass-produced and very manoeuvrable T34 tanks, some of which have been upgraded with thicker armour and a heavier gun, are more than a match for the German Panzer V tanks and Ferdinand self-propelled guns. The infantry support that the Russians have is also quite overwhelming, even though they have had a lot of casualties. They claim that they have enough troops in reserve to replace the casualties.

There are times when I could look around and ask myself just who could I trust. I've got a good wife and family, and I have other relatives and close friends that I know I can trust. But some of the soldiers that I've spoken to have wives who have been unfaithful, especially since the Americans started coming over to bases in England. Today silk stockings are a luxury item for the girls, yet the Americans seem to have them in abundance, so there are girls who have succumbed to the temptation just to get a pair of stockings.

In the Bible, as the early disciples spread their wings and took God's message further afield, it was essential that they put their trust in God to lead them and give them wisdom in their task. Jesus himself told them "Let not your hearts be troubled. Trust in God; trust also in me" (John 14:1). There are also various instances, a number of them being in the letters of St. Paul, where he writes "I have confidence in you." Like an army, we have a supreme leader in whom we can trust, but there are times when we have to have confidence and rely on each other.

49
VICTORY IN SICILY

Tuesday 31st August 1943

It's now nearly two months since Operation Husky, the invasion of Sicily, began on 10th July. The original intention was to capture the main enemy airfields by landing at a number of different points on the island simultaneously, and several plans were proposed, but in the end General Montgomery's persistence paid off. He had decided that it would be best for the British forces under his control to move up the east coast whilst American troops under General Patton covered his left flank. This could have cut off the enemy escape route across the Straits of Messina. However, Monty met stiff resistance from the German forces still in Italy, so the glory-seeking Patton advanced north, facing limited resistance from Italian troops, towards the capital, Palermo, which he entered on 23rd July, then turned east to head for the Messina.

My mother Elsie has always been a very persistent person. There were times when she really laid down the law at home, and there would be no messing about from anyone. She was a bit like our local police sergeant, who was a big burly fellow that we often saw walking the beat, watching carefully as he made his way down the town streets.

I remember when I was a child and learning to ride my new bicycle. I didn't want to go on the road because I didn't think I was quite capable enough. So, just to get a little practice, and because I couldn't see anyone around, I lifted my bicycle onto the pavement and started to ride along for a few yards. The next moment I heard a loud voice calling me from behind. Yes, it was the old police sergeant shouting at me that the pavement was for walking on, not for riding bicycles on.

There are occasions in the Bible when we read of other very persistent individuals, though their motives weren't exactly worthy. One instance is the story of Samson and Delilah. As was sometimes the case, the Israelites had done evil and turned away from God, so to punish them He committed them into the hands of the Philistines. During his life Samson, who had been blessed by God, fought a constant battle to liberate them. Unfortunately he fell in love with the Philistine girl Delilah, and Philistine officers came to her to try and persuade Samson to tell her the secret of his great strength. This she tried to do on several occasions but, after a few false examples, her persistence eventually paid off as well and Samson told her the real reason for his strength, which was his hair, which had never been cut. As soon as Delilah realised that this was the true reason she told the Philistines, who came and cut Samson's hair while he was asleep. He immediately lost his strength, and for some time he had to endure the torment of the Philistines. However, during this time his hair began to grow again, and at his death during a feast he literally brought the house down on top of the Philistines (Judges 16).

50
MUSSOLINI RESCUED

Thursday 30th September 1943

After about 6 long weeks in Russia we got back to England quite exhausted. It appears that our reports on the situation in Russia went right to the top level. However, this diplomatic life couldn't last, and I was once again posted away, this time to a replacement unit in Sicily, where the fighting in the island is dying out. Some of the new recruits still need to learn to keep their heads down, because there are still isolated pockets of resistance where they are more likely to get a sniper's bullet than a bottle of wine in their hand. The recruits seem to be getting younger all the time.

German radio reported earlier this month that German paratroopers under the command of Special Forces officer Otto Skorzeny have rescued the disgraced Italian dictator Benito Mussolini from the isolated mountain hotel on the Gran Sasso in the Apennines where he had been imprisoned. He was arrested last July when a new government under Marshal Pietro Badoglio was formed with a desire to make peace with the Allies. It appears that gliders were crash-landed near the hotel and the paratroopers soon overcame the Italian guards. Mussolini was flown to Rome, then to Germany for a meeting with Hitler.

Mussolini may have been in prison, but I don't expect he sang with the same joy as Paul and Silas did when they were released after being imprisoned in Caesarea for teaching about Christ in the city. It says that "About midnight Paul and Silas were praying and singing hymns to God, and other prisoners were listening to them. Suddenly there was such a violent earthquake that the foundations of the prison were shaken. At once all the prison doors flew open and everybody's chains came loose" (Acts 16:25-26). The jailer, who had strict instructions to guard these prisoners with his life, was about to commit suicide, but Paul and Silas called out to him not to harm himself, because all the prisoners were still there. The jailer, having realised that all this had been done with God's power, asked them how he too could be saved. Their response was to say "'Believe in the Lord Jesus, and you will be saved - you and your household" (vv. 30-31). The jailer cared for them and took them home with him, where he and his family were baptised.

When I get back I must remind the Pastor at the church that he promised to open up a new choir group. Julie admits that her musical abilities are limited, and that includes her singing talents, whereas young Bobby and I seem to have the same ideas about becoming choir members, especially since he's been taking piano lessons on mother's old honky-tonk.

51
A COMPLIMENTARY SPEECH

Sunday 31st October 1943

The RAF have been using Window, a type of metal foil strip dropped in bulk from aircraft prior to bombing raids, since last July. Its purpose is to jam enemy radar, and in doing this it has been very successful. It has certainly helped to reduce Bomber Command losses. Hermann Goering, a leading Nazi and head of the German Air Force (Luftwaffe), made an unusual speech in Berlin today. He stated "In the fields of radar [the RAF] must have the world's greatest genius. They have the geniuses and we have the nincompoops... The British would never have dared use the metal foil here if they had not worked out 100% what the antidote is. I hate the rogues like the plague, but in one respect I am obliged to doff my cap to them."

It's strange how we can dislike a person, yet still respect them for what they are. My late uncle had some very controversial views of his own about the political system in the country, and there were times when he would voice them quite openly. There were those who certainly didn't like what they heard, yet took his remarks with a pinch of salt because they knew he had been a hard-working farmer all his life, and the government's meagre provisions didn't exactly help him.

It also sounds just like the Roman governor Pontius Pilate, when he spoke to the Jews at Jesus' trial. Jesus had stood before both King Herod and Pontius Pilate, yet they found no fault in him, and Pilate echoed this when he said to the chief priests, the rulers and the people: "You brought me this man as one who was inciting the people to rebellion. I have examined him in your presence and have found no basis for your charges against him. Neither has Herod, for he sent him back to us; as you can see, he has done nothing to deserve death. Therefore, I will punish him and then release him" (Luke 21:13-16). Yet Jesus still had a task to complete, and that would only be done by his death on the cross. Perhaps it was because of Pontius Pilate's fear of the Jews that in the end he released Barabbas and allowed Jesus to be sent for crucifixion.

52
BERLIN BOMBED AGAIN

Tuesday 30th November 1943

Bomber Command has carried out more heavy raids on Berlin in another demonstration of the 'carpet' or 'saturation' bombing strategy initiated by Air Marshal Arthur 'Bomber' Harris. It appears to have slightly alarmed one of Hitler's right-hand men, the Minister of Propaganda, Josef Goebbels. Reconnaissance aircraft show the city filled with smoke and areas of fire. However, a change in the weather brought some rain, which inevitably helped to put the fires out. Much damage appears to have been caused in some of the main areas of the city, including the Wilhelmstrasse, and rubble lies everywhere. No doubt either the RAF or the US Air Force will soon be back to try and finish the job.

My Sunday School teacher always used to tell me that life is like a building made out of bricks and mortar. Our parents are the architects who bring us into life. With the help of the builders, who represent our teachers, we set the plans for the foundation of our building and take the time to ensure that the house is strong as we are taught in the ways of life, including our careers, thus laying brick upon brick as time goes by and seeing the building grow tall and strong. Yet even buildings need maintenance. During this war some of us have felt real grief, making it feel as if our lives, and thus our buildings, are falling apart. At times like that, do we stand back and hope that our house falls down quickly, or watch while there are those in the same predicament wait for their houses to fall down? I don't think so. I know my wife is always grateful for the plumber or the carpenter to come if we have a water leak or a broken chair.

In the Bible Jesus told the story of the wise and foolish builders (Matthew 7:24-29). The foolish builder had no real foundation to his house, and when the stormy weather came it fell down. This was in contrast to the wise builder, who made sure that his house was built on a firm foundation. Again, the stormy weather came, but the house remained secure. Jesus uses this story to demonstrate how Christians should dwell on our Lord's words so that, when we are confronted by opposition, we are able to use all the spiritual knowledge we have gained. He also makes it clear that we cannot rely on religious rumour or speculation that might cause us to have doubts, and stressed to the crowds that "Any kingdom divided against itself will be ruined, and a house divided against itself will fall" (Luke 11:17).

53
WHISKY GALORE!

Friday 31st December 1943

A few days ago there was a big naval engagement near Norway, when Admiral Fraser aboard his flagship, the battleship HMS *Duke of York*, intercepted and sank the enemy battleship *Scharnhorst*. However, there appears to have been one who was totally undisturbed by everything. This was the Duke of York's feline mascot, a tabby cat named Whisky. It is said that he slept through the whole battle! It's nice to hear of those who have complete confidence in the crew to get on with their job, which they did with great success.

It was just like our two black cats at home, who were very affectionate and very trusting. If they knew I was there the smaller one, Polly, would rub herself against my legs until I picked her up. Once that was done she would climb up on my shoulder and lick my left ear, then climb contentedly back into my arms to curl up for a while. The larger one, Joey, tended to be more of an outdoor cat, but in the evening he would always come in if I gave him a call. He always enjoyed passing the night lying along my legs, where he would feel the warmth from my body and expect a little stroke whilst he was there.

At a time when Christianity was spreading, the apostle Paul gave his support to some of the new churches that were being created, but he couldn't be there all the time. He had to rely on their desire to be faithful. He wrote to the church in Corinth "I have great confidence in you; I take great pride in you. I am greatly encouraged; in all our troubles my joy knows no bounds" (2 Cor. 7:4). Yet who should we have most confidence in? Is it our church, our chaplain, or someone else? As Christians we can have full confidence in only one person, and that is God himself. He has confidence in us and if we are obedient to Him then, as it is written in the letter to the Hebrews, "Therefore, brothers, since we have confidence to enter the Most Holy Place by the blood of Jesus, by a new and living way opened for us through the curtain, that is, his body, and since we have a great high priest over the house of God, let us draw near to God with a sincere heart in full assurance of faith, having our hearts sprinkled to cleanse us from a guilty conscience and having our bodies washed with pure water" (Hebrews 10:19-22).

1944

54
COUNTER-ATTACKS
AT ANZIO

Monday 31st January 1944

My uniform's wet and cold, and I've had to deal with nothing but mud and snow in my boots over the last three months. We've all had the same problem. Many of us are exhausted not just from hunger and the lack of sleep, but also from the task of having to clean our clothes almost daily. When hot water's available we use anything from helmets to tin baths to do the cleaning. I saw one American GI boil his socks in his helmet, but how he got them dry afterwards I do not know.

Meanwhile, on 22nd January there was news of landings near the Italian port of Anzio as part of a combined group made up of the British and American forces under the command of General Lucas. Unfortunately over a week was wasted making sure the bridgehead was secure, and there was no progress inland at all. Over that time Field Marshal Kesselring was able to regroup his forces and has now launched a counter-attack against the bridgehead. Even so, with the forces we have available we are confident that we will be able to withstand the enemy attacks. It was just a shame that the enemy ended up in such a readily camouflaged area. We knew where they had been, but none of our reconnaissance patrols could see them in their new positions.

Julie wrote and said how she'd been looking after the children of a lord of the manor, who lived in his large house a short distance out of town, along the country lanes. He has a large orchard at the back of the house, which goes back to Tudor times. His wife very kindly gave Julie an apple pie for her services. The gardener was saying that other children had been stealing some of the apples, no doubt because of the food rationing, but he added with a smile that they were very sour Granny Smith cooking apples. Any child who ate them before running away was likely to end up with a very nasty tummy ache. The lord of the manor himself did not wish to accuse anyone of theft, particularly small children. He felt that their tummy ache would act as a deterrent, if not a punishment, in itself.

When we accept Jesus Christ as our Saviour, we are unlikely to be ignored by satanic forces, which can be very subtle. Jesus himself was tempted in the same way during his time on earth. Satan tried to offer him power over the world, he tried to force Jesus to do miracles at his time of hunger in order to feed himself, and to demonstrate his divine power through a suicidal act. Each time Jesus answered in the same way, quoting the Scriptures every time (Matthew 4:1-11). In this way Christ was able to resist Satan, and the devil just gave up. It is written that "The devil left him, and angels came and attended him" (v.11). Let us do likewise, so we can move forward in our ministry.

55
FIRST U-BOATS FITTED
WITH A SCHNORCHEL

Tuesday 29th February 1944

Due to the intensity of our air attacks, U-Boats have been seen using a new device, called the snorkel (German 'Schnorchel'). We believe it to be a development of the air mast fitted experimentally to Dutch submarines in 1933. When raised it supplies air to the submarine's diesel motors whilst automatically expelling exhaust gases, which allows the submarine to remain underwater for longer periods. However, we also believe that there is one major problem. Most submarines have to surface to take a sighting and establish their position, which is usually calculated by the captain every four hours or so. If the submarine has to remain underwater for longer, then it is much more likely to stray from the planned course, because in the darkness underwater it cannot determine its true position. One U-Boat prisoner told us that their boat had inadvertently strayed into a minefield.

To be honest, I don't think this is a new idea but an old idea that's been adapted for use on a machine. I always think of Bobby and how he's doing with his swimming, and I remember when he used to break off a small piece of hollow reed from the bank. If he kept this in his mouth he found he could breathe underwater. He sometimes used it to look down towards the bottom of the pool, no doubt hoping that he might find buried treasure. He never found the treasure he was looking for, but the enjoyment and curiosity of it led him to do it again and again.

How do we, as Christians, establish that we are still moving along the way that God has planned for us? Through our lives we can demonstrate the characteristics that God wants from us - understanding, honesty, fairness, truth, hope, and righteousness. That comes on top of our continuing faith and prayer. These were all demonstrated by our Lord Jesus when he walked the earth. John, one of Jesus' original disciples, wrote: "This is the message we have heard from him (Jesus) and declare to you. God is light, in Him there is no darkness at all. If we claim to have fellowship with Him yet walk in the darkness, we lie and do not live by the truth. But if we walk in the light, as He is in the light, we have fellowship with one another, and the blood of Jesus, His Son, purifies us from all sin" (1 John 1:5-7). He later adds "This is how we know we are in Him: Whoever claims to live in Him must walk as Jesus did" (vv. 7-8). To live in Him is to walk in His way.

56
THE GREAT ESCAPE

Friday 31st March 1944

A mass escape has been carried out by Allied officers imprisoned at Stalag Luft III, the German prisoner-of-war camp at Sagan, a town with a population of about 25,000 in the lower class region of Silesia, about halfway between Berlin and Breslau, and run by the Luftwaffe. The camp, made up of the usual numerous wooden barrack room huts and surrounded by a double-layered barbed wire fence, was originally set up towards the Polish border, and a great distance from any friendly or neutral territory.

However, according to the latest German propaganda bulletins, these escapers did not have much success. Because of the numbers that had to be used to seek out the escapers, once the storm had broken, Hitler gave a personal order stating that at least 50 of the escapers were to be shot on recapture. This appears to have been carried out without hesitation. Though a lot of confusion was certainly created amongst the enemy soldiers, we don't yet know if there were any who made it to freedom. A number have already been returned to Stalag Luft III. All this certainly caused problems for the prisoners of war over there, but if Hitler thinks he wants to deter any further escapes by demonstrating what his black uniformed bullies can do, then he needs to think again!

The evacuation of the British army from Dunkirk took place at the end of May 1940, when many of our lads were taken prisoner because they were left as part of the perimeter forces. Their job was to stop, or at least delay the advance of all the enemy tanks and infantry into the town until the evacuation had taken place, a job which they did with great courage. Since then our high-ups have always impressed upon us the importance of being able to do one's duty, even as a prisoner of war, and they all consider it the soldier's duty to escape. There have been a few discussions in the camp about this. My company is made up of a mixed bunch, half of which are quite literate or well spoken, the other half is made up of a bunch of reformed crooks, but they all have a part to play. My Sergeant James is one of the former group, and speaks several languages fluently. He has offered to give language lessons in both German and French. One private, whom everyone knows as Slick Jack, admits to have been an expert forger during his criminal life, so he has offered to give a few lessons in this. There was, of course, one condition. He showed me an identity card that he had recently forged for a friend. I must admit, it really looks like the real thing. He told me that so long as I kept quiet about the identity card, then he would be willing to give lessons or hints as to how to make maps or identity documents.

As Christians we have an escape route, but we must be willing to let God guide us. In talking about the duties of workmen who are approved of God, the apostle Paul writes to Timothy "Those who oppose him he must gently instruct, in the hope that God will grant them repentance leading them to a knowledge of the truth, and that they will come to their senses and escape from the trap of the devil, who has taken them captive to do his will" (2 Timothy 2:25-26).

57

A SEA OF DESPAIR

Sunday 30th April 1944

Around some of the nearby areas in Devon where many of the American forces are based there is almost a sense of foreboding. Something has gone very wrong, but no-one quite knows what it is. In the town that my friends Jack and Penny visited last week there are already rumours going around. You have one neighbour claiming that radio reports have indicated the success of a particular mission, and on the other side you have a neighbour who says that the newspaper reports seem to indicate that the same raid was a failure. Whom does one believe? Any such rumours can also arouse fear, and this is why we like to get to the bottom of things and quell any wild or imaginary rumours. Rumours can be a very difficult thing to deal with.

There must have been orders not to reveal any information, because the American soldiers congregating in the local public houses are just too scared to say anything, other than admitting to some loss of life. However, there are indications that this may have been a rehearsal for the planned invasion that we all know can't be too far ahead. Any of the big Devon beaches could have been used to give the soldiers their first taste of battlefield experience. Shooting at a dummy is one thing, but to get your feet wet by jumping off a landing craft for the first time with someone firing back at you is another. There's always a limit to how far you can go. A soldier can never quite understand fear until he faces the real thing. Whether the weather conditions were considered is unsure, because anyone aboard a landing craft in rough waters in this awful weather would soon wish they had never volunteered. We know that training up to now has had to be as realistic as possible. Anyone can be told to charge towards the layers of barbed wire on the ground, and then to crawl under them, but it's not so easy when bullets are flying past your ear!

When the early missionaries went out to spread the gospel they didn't get the opportunity to rehearse. They merely went out in faith. At the time there was much persecution from the Romans, who saw the worship of many gods as part of their traditional life. Others, to whose nature Christianity was contrary, also made trouble. The first apostle to give his life was Stephen, who, having borne witness publicly to the Jews of their sin, was stoned by them outside Jerusalem (Acts 7:54-60). Later on, some of Jesus' own disciples would be put on trial for their beliefs. It is said that one particular example of this was to be Simon Peter who, unlike the Lord Jesus, chose to be crucified upside down because it would more shameful to him. Many others were to give their lives during the persecution that followed, but no doubt many lives were saved because of their teaching.

58
MONTE CASSINO TAKEN

Wednesday 31st May 1944

Ever since Italy signed the surrender documents last September we have had to deal with the retreating German forces. They recognised the problems that we would face advancing through the mountains that run up the spine of Italy. They therefore prepared concealed defensive positions across the Italian mainland. Our forces were split by the Italian mountains, so the high monastery of Monte Cassino proved to be an excellent observation post for the enemy. On several occasions we tried to assault the big walled monastery fortress on top of the cliff, but in the end we had to resort to the air force, which sent many B-17 bombers to simply level the place. It is understood that the monastery held many antique Christian scrolls, so we have yet to discover what happened to them, and whether they were removed or destroyed in the bombing.

I remember how we used to go for long walks on Saturdays into the Welsh mountains. We always laid out a base camp, and the person we would rely on to do our catering when we got back would stay there. This was usually my wife or sister-in-law, both of whom coped very well with our old Primus stove. When we got back we were often a little exhausted, and those of us who took part were always grateful to have a good dish of food and a cup of tea ready. Makes a change to what we get after all our long marches today, especially when supplies are low. When we have to dig into our emergency rations we usually find that the hard biscuits in the tin just get harder and harder every day. As for Spam, and more Spam - yuk!

Unfortunately, this last month, I've really begun to feel the strain of responsibility on active duty here in Italy. I've become touchy, jumpy and ill-tempered, which is totally unlike me. Even our doctor has noticed it. It's his job to keep everyone in the pink of condition, but deep down he's as understanding a friend as one could have. The CO gave me 72 hours' leave, and appeared to have earmarked me for "other duties", though what he meant by that I wasn't sure. I had some army pay saved up, so I took the train down to Taranto, a port on the heel of the country that I had never visited before. It's where the RAF carried out a surprise raid on the Italian fleet back in November 1940.

When I did get back to base on 28th May the CO showed me a request he had just received from top brass. They urgently needed someone who could act as both interrogator and translator at one of the big Italian prisoner of war camps in the Midlands. They were looking for a no-nonsense man with suitable language skills who could deal with the Italian prisoners whilst discreetly reading their thoughts. I must have some of those talents, because the CO recommended me right away. I'm due to leave in two days' time. The job will have its advantages, one of these being that I will be able to see the family more. I haven't spent any decent time with them for months, so it will be good to see how life is treating them. I will also get full promotion to the rank of Major.

There are those who believe that once they are baptised, then everything is done and dusted, and their place in heaven is guaranteed. But God doesn't want our lives or our thoughts to be based on a one-off event. God want us to pursue Him every day, to build on what His desires are, to create a Christian fortress in our lives that He can be proud of. Our faith and trust in Him should be revealed in our obedience to Him every day of our lives. The apostle Paul writes: "Those who live according to the sinful nature have their minds set on what that nature desires, but those who live in accordance with the Spirit have their minds set on what the Spirit desires" (Romans 8:5). We all make mistakes, but we have an understanding, compassionate and forgiving God to whom we can turn at any time for help, guidance, and a spiritual strength to lead us on. Paul confirms this when he adds "You, however, are controlled not by the sinful nature, but by the Spirit, if the Spirit of God lives I you. And if anyone does not have the Spirit of Christ, he does not belong to Christ. But if Christ is in you, your body is dead because of sin, yet your spirit is alive because of righteousness. And if the Spirit of him who raised Jesus from the dead is living in you, he who raised Christ from the dead will also give life to your mortal bodies through his Spirit, who lives in you" (Romans 8:9-11).

59
OPERATION OVERLORD – OR IS IT?

Friday 30th June 1944

It was announced on 6th June that Allied forces had landed on the beaches of France. For a while there was much said about whether the landings in Normandy are the real thing, or whether it is just a feint attack to draw enemy troops there so that the main landing could take place elsewhere, probably in the Pas de Calais region. This was the most obvious area to land on, simply because it is closest to the English shore. Many small-scale rubber dummies, dressed in paratrooper's uniforms, were dropped from aircraft in set areas. The American dummies are very lifelike, and are built to explode with the effect of gunfire on striking the ground, thus attracting the attention of enemy forces. The Americans call them 'dolls', but we have given them the name 'Rupert'. There have also been a lot of radio messages from the First US Army Group (FUSAG), under the most effective tank commander General George Patton, based near Dover, whom the Germans believe will lead the main assault on land.

My father always told me as a child to "expect the unexpected", because one day the unexpected will turn up. It's possible that the enemy may have ignored this simple proverb, because all their tank reserves appear to have been grouped the Northern France, near the Pas de Calais.

As Christians we too need to make sure that we are not deceived by those around us who do not believe in Christ. The apostle Paul had two special pieces of advice for believers in the city of Colossus. The first are "no one may deceive you by fine-sounding arguments" (Col. 2:4) and "See to it that no one takes you captive through hollow and deceptive philosophy, which depend on human tradition and the basic principles of this world rather than on Christ" (Col. 2:8). We need to keep looking to God. Remember, one Lord, one Faith, one Baptism.

60
BOMB PLOT

Monday 31st July 1944

For months people around here have been asking why a mission is not carried out to eliminate Hitler. I would think that question has often been asked elsewhere. After all, he is the one who started this war. It is rumoured that the Prime Minister was even considering a plan to send a commando group to attack Hitler at his command centre. Questions have been asked as to why this has not been done, but I suspect that Hitler has made a number of tactical mistakes since he declared himself to be the Commander-in-Chief of all German forces. If the Germans had any choice they would probably have allowed command to rest with their most experienced officers and, by doing this, hindered our efforts to bring this war to an end.

The German news broadcasts on 20th July reported that there had been an attempt on the Fuehrer's life during one of his regular conferences at the so-called 'Wolf's Lair' in Bavaria. The bomb was activated by one of those present, who then left on the pretence that he had received a telephone call recalling him to Berlin, a call which was made by one of the other conspirators. Though several other high-ranking officers were killed, and others injured, Hitler himself suffered few injuries, and in his anger he announced that any officers found to have been directly or indirectly linked to the plot would face trial and execution. Hitler later declared that he was a "divine person" not to have been killed. Others believe that the table over which he must have been standing somehow shielded him from the blast.

When we try making out that we are divine, we are asking for trouble. As we go back through history we read of those who have won great victories in battle, or done marvellous feats, and some of those called themselves divine. The only similarity between them now is that they are all dead. At least, most of them. The only exception is the Lord Jesus Christ, God's Son. In His death on the cross at Calvary He bore the sin of all mankind, but He was resurrected, and today our Saviour and Redeemer sits triumphant at the right hand of God.

61
LIBERATION OF PARIS

Thursday 31st August 1944

It has been reported that Lt-General von Choltitz, the German commander in Paris, has surrendered to the Allied forces, without carrying out Hitler's order to destroy the city. Many of the occupying troops had left, so their commander declared Paris an open city. The commander of the Free French forces, General Charles de Gaulle, took great pride in walking with his forces down the Champs Elysées, taking little notice of any distant shots still being fired by the isolated pockets of German resistance who had ignored the order to surrender. De Gaulle was presented with gifts of flowers, and acknowledged the cheers of the Parisians along the way, many of whom loudly sang 'La Marseillaise', the French national anthem. Even so, the French population is still busy rounding up many collaborators, to whom they have shown little mercy. French women who sided with enemy soldiers in Paris are being driven down the streets in dirty trucks, and have then had to endure the humiliating experience of having their heads shaven.

I suppose I'm one of those very traditional, very patriotic Britons, and I can't imagine how I would feel if Julie suddenly walked off as a collaborator. I know it's one of those things that one can only picture in one's mind, and I just wouldn't be able to understand it all. I expect there are a good few Frenchmen who are thinking just like that at the moment. When I think about it, even children can lose their temper if they find that someone has been telling tales on them. Learning to deal with it in the right way is all part of the growing-up process.

It sounds similar to Jesus Christ's entry into Jerusalem. Many had heard of His wonderful deeds, and when He rode into the city on the back of a donkey many people lining the route "spread their cloaks on the road, while others cut branches from the trees and spread them on the road" (Matthew 21:8). Yet Christ, unlike de Gaulle, did not enter the city with the intention of being glorified by the people in order to satisfy his pride and boost his ego. Christ's glory was to come later, on the humble cross of Calvary.

62
THE REVENGE WEAPONS

Saturday 30th September 1944

All this month the population of London has had to endure the latest of Hitler's so-called 'Miracle' or 'Revenge' weapons. The V-1 flying bombs, referred to as the Doodlebugs, started coming over last June, only a couple of weeks after D-Day. The first day alone we had six hit London. They are fast, and our fighters had great difficulty catching them. The one suggestion was that fighters should position themselves way above the expected altitude for the Doodlebugs, and then dive down behind them and open fire. The only problem here was that some pilots opened fire at too close a range and then the missile would explode right in front of them, which caused damage to the following fighter. However, one pilot rather took the initiative and, instead of opening fire on the missile, he guided the wing of his aircraft underneath that of the missile. By increasing his altitude gradually by a few feet, he was then able to tip the missile over. This probably disrupted the gyro system which was being used to guide the missile, and sent it plummeting to the ground.

However, now we have to deal with the V-2 as well, which is powered by a new rocket motor. These have a much longer range than the V-1s, so they can be launched from within Germany. Unfortunately for us they are so fast that we get no warning of them at all. The one-ton high-explosive warhead not only causes a big bang but sends strong shock waves out that cause great structural damage to any buildings in the area. Because there is no warning, there has already been considerable loss of life because people aren't able to get under cover quick enough.

Whilst in London, Julie has been frightened by the sight of the V-1s that come over regularly, but she's been lucky, because they seem to be aimed for central London rather than the northern area of the city where she works part-time. During Julie's work hours Bobby is looked after by some of her friends, who have children of their own. Julie has also seen the shortage of gun crew on the many anti-aircraft guns that have been transferred to the coast in an effort to bring down these pilotless missiles, and has considered taking a training course in gunnery so she can play a more active part. It's certainly one idea, but it all depends on both how long the training takes, and also for how long we might have to put up with them. If we can get our fast fighters into the air in good time, then we will stand a better chance of bringing them down, rather on having to rely on a random box barrage by the anti-aircraft guns, which hasn't been very successful up to now.

This may be an unseen weapon, but I'm glad we have an unseen friend. Early in His ministry on earth Jesus said "When you pray, go into your room, close the door and pray to your Father, who is unseen. Then your Father, who sees what is done in secret, will reward you" (Matthew 6:6). We may not see all the dangers around us, or know how to deal with them yet, but God our Father does. I'm sure that as we look to Him then we may also rely on God's Holy Spirit to guide us.

63
RETURN TO THE PHILIPPINES

Tuesday 31st October 1944

There have been some big naval engagements around the Philippine Islands. We had deceived the Japanese by landing at Leyte, rather than going straight for Manila, the capital. In the Battle of Leyte Gulf there have been losses on both sides, but the bulk of the Japanese fleet, including their giant battleship Musashi, has been sent to the bottom. Our carrier pilots have done a good job! One thing we didn't expect was Japanese suicide pilots, or Kamikaze (meaning 'Divine Wind'). Their old planes are packed with high explosive, and the pilots dive straight in onto our ships, causing heavy damage.

A few days ago General Macarthur kept his promise to the people of the Philippines when he stepped off a landing craft and waded ashore, followed by several photographers. He had promised that he would return, and announced in his speech "People of the Philippines, I have returned. By the grace of Almighty God our forces stand again on Philippine soil - soil consecrated in the blood of our two peoples… rally to me."

It's now been six months since I started this job at the PoW camp. Most of the Italians can see that the war will be over soon, and some of them are making plans for the future. I get on well with them, and they have shared stories of their own families back in Italy, as well as asking me for help with their problems, some of which I've been able to assist with. Even the food is fair, and whenever I can I try to put something by to take home. It may not be much, but from what Julie tells me it's all well received. She is always asking me in her letters if I have any idea when I might visit them again. There are times when I have to reply quite truthfully, if a little regretfully, that I just don't know. At the moment it's nothing but a dream - one minute the idea and the optimism are there, then it's all too suddenly gone again.

If a mere general can keep such a promise to return, how can we not believe that our Lord and Saviour Jesus Christ will keep His promise to return? Before His arrest, Jesus knew that the disciples were not only concerned about Him, but worried that after He had gone they would not know what to do. Jesus tried to reassure them, saying "Do not let your hearts be troubled. Trust in God, trust also in me. In my Father's house are many rooms; if it were not so, I would have told you. I am going there to prepare a place for you. And if I go and prepare a place for you, I will come back and take you to be with me that you also may be where I am" (John 14:1-3). However, at an earlier point in his ministry, when Jesus again was considering His return, He reminded the disciples "You also must be ready, because the Son of Man will come at an hour when you do not expect him" (Luke 12:40). No man knows the day nor the hour, but are we ready to receive Him when He comes again?

64
TIRPITZ SUNK!

Thursday 30th November 1944

News came through earlier this month that the mighty battleship *Tirpitz*, which displaced 42,900 tons and was a sister ship of the *Bismarck*, has been sunk in Norwegian waters by Lancaster bombers from 617 (renowned as the

Dambuster squadron) and nine squadrons of the RAF carrying the big 12,000 lb Tallboy or 'Earthquake' bombs. *Tirpitz*, with her main armament of 8x15 inch guns, had been a constant threat to all our Arctic convoys heading for Russia, and a number of our warships had been put on the alert in case she turned up. Several raids had been made by miniature submarines of the Royal Navy and aircraft of Bomber Command on the Tirpitz since 1941, but this time the ship took several direct hits, as well as a few near misses, and the overall damage caused by the direct hits, together with the shock waves caused by the near misses, resulted in her capsizing in Tromsø Fjord.

In her latest letter Julie has told me that some of the boys round the park near our home had their own way of re-enacting this sinking. They cut out a big wooden plank and drilled out a couple of holes in the top half to represent masts. They then glued on a funnel shaped section and added a couple of small blocks at each end to represent the gun turrets. After adding a bit of weight to the bottom half in order to keep their model upright, they let it go in the small stream that leads to the nearby lake. They then waited on the small bridge across the stream so they could drop small stones or other missiles onto the model battleship as it floated underneath. One of the boys always waited toward the end of the stream so they could recover their target and have another go at sinking it. Such imagination!

It's almost like the story of the disciples in the upper room. Suddenly they were overcome by a mighty wind as the power of the Holy Spirit moved over them. It is written that "When the day of Pentecost came, they were all together in one place. Suddenly a sound like the blowing of a violent wind came from heaven and filled the whole house where they were sitting. They saw what seemed to be tongues of fire that separated and came to rest on each of them. All of them were filled with the Holy Spirit and began to speak in other tongues as the Spirit enabled them" (Acts 2:1-4). The nearby crowd were divided - some were amazed, whilst others thought they were merely drunk. For this reason Peter stood up, and in his speech to the crowd he included the words "I will show wonders in the heaven above, and signs on the earth below, blood and fire and billows of smoke. The sun will be turned to darkness and the moon to blood before the coming of the great and glorious day of the Lord. And everyone who calls on the name of the Lord will be saved" (Acts 2:19-21). After the Holy Spirit came upon him Peter certainly knew how to get the message of the Lord through!

65
GLENN MILLER MISSING

Sunday 31st December 1944

Julie and her friends have talked about some of the entertainment they regularly enjoy in the nearby village hall. This is large and, whilst being the venue for the local art club and bridge club, it is of quite adequate size to fit in a small band to which they can dance. USO (United Services Organizations) is the American equivalent of the British ENSA (Entertainments National Service Association), and many celebrities like Bob Hope, Marlene Dietrich, George Formby and Vera Lynn ('the forces Sweetheart') have been attached to it. Bandleader Glenn Miller is famous for playing songs like *Chattanooga Choo-Choo* and *In The Mood*. He and his band were due to entertain the troops in Paris, so Miller took a flight across the Channel to France on 14th December. Unfortunately it seems he disappeared during the flight, and no trace of him or the plane has been found. The weather was quite bad, and if he made it to France it's possible that he could have landed unexpectedly at one of the local airfields to refuel, but the signs aren't good.

It can be hard to lose a friend. My mother has written to me expressing her concern for my young sister Jane. Jane is married to another Robert, who was called up in late 1940. He joined the RAF and, because of his experience with all the mechanised equipment that they have on their farm, he was taken on as an RAF Maintenance Engineer. He was posted to Malta in March 1941, where they did a grand job, not only keeping all the fighters in the air, but keeping all the essential vehicles around the airfields well serviced, particularly because of the shortage of spares. However, Robert was sitting with his two good friends Dusty and Skinny in a tent on one of the main inland airfields. Those two lads also lived near us in Worthing, so I knew them well.

Suddenly they had warning of another air raid. Mother says that Robert needed to go outside for a moment to relieve himself, when a flight of black Heinkel He-111 medium bombers suddenly flew over at low altitude. He rushed to take cover, but fell and sprained his wrist when he felt the shock from a sudden explosion. When he returned he found fragments of the tent scattered everywhere around a giant bomb crater in the ground, but of his friends, and mine, there was nothing.

They bandaged up Robert's left wrist as best they could in the 90th General Hospital on the island, but I'm sure it will take us both a while to get over the haunting shock of what actually happened in that short moment of time. By His grace God had certainly spared Robert's life, but not the lives of our friends. Life can be hell sometimes and, even as a Christian, it really makes you ask why God allows us to undergo such grief and fear. There are times when I wish I could perform miracles, and bring my friends back from the dead, simply because of the emptiness that one feels after such a loss.

The same happened to the disciples after Jesus had been crucified. They too were upset, because Jesus had been such a great part of their lives, and to have him no longer was quite overwhelming. Yet after He had risen from the dead on the third day, Christ appeared to the disciples on several occasions. At the time of the Ascension, we read that "When (Jesus) had lead them out to the vicinity of Bethany, he lifted up his hands and blessed them. While he was blessing them, he left them and was taken into heaven. Then they worshipped him and returned to Jerusalem with great joy. And they stayed continually at the temple, praising God" (Luke 24:50-53). It can be hard to accept that someone we love is no longer with us, but we have a great heavenly comforter.

1945

66
THE BATTLE OF THE BULGE

Wednesday 31st January 1945

Last month my parents had got the idea that the war might be over by Christmas, so they invited us all up for a long weekend just so that we could celebrate Christmas together. However, on 16th December, just when I was planning to get some leave, we had some alarming news from the front. Unknown to us, Hitler had amassed many infantry and tank divisions in the Ardennes forest in Belgium. This area was only thinly held by American troops because it was believed that being thickly wooded, it was impenetrable to motorised forces. We were proved wrong!

The enemy objective was the recapture of Antwerp, which would deny the Allies an essential supply base and also split the British and American forces in two. Initially we suffered severe losses, and the misty conditions on the ground meant that we could not make any sort of air strike against the tanks. However, because the enemy were relying very much on the capture of our fuel dumps we were able to hold him, but we were fortunate in denying him this luxury. It appears that a number of enemy paratroopers were dropped in American army uniforms. Their intention was to ensure that the bridges across the Meuse River were not destroyed by our retreating forces, whilst causing the maximum amount of confusion by resetting signposts.

Initially they were very successful in doing so, and many of our troops found themselves lost. Once the weather had cleared our fighter-bombers were able to take off and take rich pickings on the enemy force, including the many armoured vehicles that had been gathered together in the Ardennes for this last-ditch assault.

All types of weather are to be found in the Scriptures. Most of us know about the heavy rain that caused the flood in Noah's time, but there are other references to storms, wind, sun and even snow. God spoke to Job out of a storm (Job 38:1), and it was a storm in the Adriatic Sea that brought Paul to Malta. Sometimes our lives can be in a bit of a storm, but the apostle James writes: "When he asks (for wisdom), he must believe and not doubt, because he who doubts is like a wave of the sea, blown and tossed by the wind" (James 1:6). Do we have any doubt what God can do?

67
RUSSIAN OFFENSIVE

Wednesday 28th February 1945

It's still pretty cold over here and, apart from the restrictions on fuel and water, my Julie has had difficulty getting any decent new warm clothes for our son. We can't afford anything too expensive, and anything in the local market gets snapped up quite promptly. She is having to get out some of her mother Pearl's old clothes and get onto her sewing machine to see if she can not only update them a little, but try and make them fit. Pearl is of a rather large size, so it would be a waste of time trying them on as they are, because they just wouldn't fit, and would look awful.

Even though the weather can't be much different, the Russians have launched their offensive in the east only days after the Battle of the Bulge. They have now advanced over 250 miles and liberated much of Poland. This included the coal fields and industrial areas of Silesia, which the enemy had occupied for all its resources. Marshal Zhukov, who is commanding the central forces, is now approaching the Oder river and can be no more than about 45 miles from Berlin. However, due to heavy casualties it is possible that the Russians will regroup and consolidate their position, which they will do once they occupy some of the areas that were bypassed during this major advance.

The apostle Paul initially made his journey to Jerusalem with the intention of persecuting Christians, but after his conversion on the road to Damascus he pushed on and helped spread the gospel to many different areas through his missionary work. But it didn't stop there. Paul wrote 13 letters in the New Testament, both to the new churches in cities where he had been and to personal friends. At all times he provided encouragement when things were going well or support when times were hard or if they faced problems. Even when he was taken as a prisoner to Rome, Paul, because he was a Roman citizen, was allowed the freedom to write letters from there, and continued to exalt God through all his letters.

68
ACROSS THE RHINE

Saturday 31st March 1945

American troops have now crossed the Rhine, considered to be the main barrier to advancing troops. The latest reports say that they met surprisingly little resistance from an enemy force made up of youngsters, probably conscripted from the Hitler Youth, and older men. It's as if they weren't expecting us at all! We later found maps that showed that they expected us to cross some 10 miles to the south. When interrogated one soldier mentioned that they had been given reports of a lot of action to the south. I wonder if they have been deceived in the same way as they were before Operation Overlord.

My relations have been enjoying themselves near my father's riverside house. My young son Bobby in particular looks forward to going swimming, though whether he will brave the cold to do that I'm not sure. It's still only early spring, and he may find that the water is still a little too cold for comfort. I'm sure that some children adapt quite well to the temperature around them, but it's not something I would want to do too often.

There's an old saying, "Once bitten, twice shy", which can often apply to our Christian lives. As simple human beings we can never be perfect. The Israelites in the Scriptures were just the same. They worshipped God one minute, then the next they found there was an idol they could see, so they turned round to worship that. It certainly wasn't what God wanted, and there are times when He had to punish them. But they were still His people, and through His love He tried to bring them back into the way of righteousness. If we stray, then find that what we have done is wrong, we can always look to God, for He is a forgiving God. But would we go and do the same thing again? I hope not.

69
DEATH OF A PRESIDENT

Monday 30th April 1945

On the 10th April it was reported that the American President, Franklin Delano Roosevelt, had died. This was his fourth term as President, and it was well known that he had been suffering for a long time from severe polio. He looked quite weak when he, Churchill and Stalin met at Yalta in January. Roosevelt had instigated the Lend/Lease plan to help supply Britain with food and arms during the early days of the war, much of which was very much appreciated by the military forces and the civilian population.

Roosevelt was of strong character, and hated to be thought of as crippled for life whilst still in office. He had had to make speeches in front of Congress and when he visited other areas of the country, speeches were made to the people of America who were present. Rather than have people see him with a walking-stick, he would prepare himself at the podium in advance, and keep a support there if he found it essential.

It's rather like my grandfather; he began to use a stick more and more in later life, but he would always use it very discreetly during some of the public meetings he attended, or even if he went out to the theatre, which was one of his favourite hobbies. He was a past president of the local drama group, and maintained close contact with the actors all the time. He would have been the first to tell us what the next production was to be!

Had Jesus been around I'm sure Roosevelt would have got his friends to lower him down through the roof to seek healing, just as they did for the paralytic (Luke 5:17-20). Even so, with the many wounded coming back from the battlefields, whose responsibility should we say they are? Our local cottage hospital is full of those who have lost limbs, or are suffering from other diseases inflicted upon them by this war. Many suffer from psychological illness, or what we tend to call shell shock, something which in the past was treated with some contempt, rather like cowardice. Whatever their individual problem may be, they all need friends. Are we likely to ignore them?

Jesus told the parable of the good Samaritan, when an ordinary man found himself assaulted and left on the side of the road, too weak to help himself. Three men walked past, but only one of them, a Samaritan, stopped to treat the injured man's wounds, and then took him on his own donkey to an inn, where he paid for the man's room as well as any other care he might need. Jesus tried to emphasise the effort that had been put into this, so he chose the Samaritan because he belonged to a tribe that the Jews hated. He then asked "Which of these three do you think was a neighbour to the man who fell into the hands of robbers?" The expert in the law replied, 'The one who had mercy on him.' Jesus told him, 'Go and do likewise'" (Luke 11:25-37). If a man who came from a tribe looked upon with some contempt by the Jews could show such mercy, then why could the Jews not show the same mercy themselves?

70
VE DAY

Thursday 31st May 1945

At the beginning of May German radio broadcast that Hitler had died in Berlin, while Mussolini has come to a sticky end in Italy, his body having been hung upside down with that of his mistress, Clara Petacci, in the main square in Milan. That's the end of the dreams of worldwide empires lasting 1000 years.

On 4th May an unconditional surrender document for German forces in north-west Germany, the Netherlands and Denmark, including some of the Scandinavian islands, was drawn up and signed by high-ranking German officers in the presence of Field Marshal Montgomery at Luneburg

Heath. However the Russian leader, Josef Stalin, refused to recognize this document, saying that there had been no Russian officers there to witness the surrender terms. For this reason the process was repeated on 7th May, when officers of the German High Command, led by Field Marshal Keitel, signed the form of unconditional surrender.

The following day here in London, people were all over the streets celebrating, and many rushed to the railings surrounding Buckingham Palace calling for the King to appear. He appeared most graciously on the balcony at the Palace at around midday with the Queen and the two royal princesses. Also present with them was Prime Minister Winston Churchill, who appeared with his traditional cigar, giving his famous V-for-Victory sign. No doubt many similar celebrations have taking place right through the country. This has been a long war, so my family are pleased that the conflict is finally drawing to an end.

I know the war against Japan still has to be ended, but everything seems a little strange. Our time as soldiers is nearly over, and some time next month we may go along to the main hall to be demobbed, pick up a suit, hat, shoes and a few other necessities and then we'll be back on the streets as civilians. Everything has changed so much over the last five years, it's hard to picture what life will be like in the future. Nor do any of us really know how long it might take for things to get back to a reasonably normal situation.

I suppose it's much the same feeling that Simon Peter had when Jesus called him as one of the first disciples. He may have been a little apprehensive, but it is written that the four fishermen, James, John, Simon Peter and Andrew, "pulled their boats up on shore, left everything and followed him" (Luke 5:11). They had heard Jesus teach, they had seen him heal many, and they had been the ones to whom Jesus revealed his power by telling them to cast their nets out, after which they brought in a totally unexpectedly large catch of fish. They may not have been fully prepared for what lay ahead, but they had all seen Jesus' power and recognised that he was someone very special. After the large catch, even Peter went to Jesus and humbly said "Go away from me, Lord. I am a sinful man". But Jesus reassured him, saying "Don't be afraid, from now on you will catch men" (vv. 8-10). Just like the disciples, we may not know what lies ahead, and we may not have had the privilege of meeting Jesus face to face, but through our faith, our regular communication with Him through prayer, and our obedience to His Word, so He will lead us in the way we should go.

POST-WAR THOUGHTS

In June, once my war had ended, I got back home one sunny day to a hearty welcome from my family, but even they had changed. Julie has a new career planned, and Bobby has grown to be a bright young teenager during the five years I've been in uniform. Unfortunately some of my friends weren't so lucky; they didn't make it back. The country itself has changed, and there's a new government in power. We also have to deal with the scores of Axis prisoners still over here. It looks like some of them, particularly the Italians, have even decided to stay and make a go of things for themselves in this country, though how difficult they might find it I just don't know. It all depends upon whether people want to hold grudges or not.

As for my life as a Christian, that has also matured. Over the last five years I've seen those in dire need, and those who have been given more than they expected. When I started this diary I thought it would last no more than a few months, but over these five years of conflict it has come to mean something special to me. It's been my way of looking at life and events as they happened, then looking at those events and expressing my thoughts upon how they reflect upon my Christian life. It's given me a real understanding of what human character can be like, from the hate on one side to the dedication and commitment on the other. With that understanding I'm sure I'll be able to pursue my wish to live out my life for Christ, wherever God would have me. God bless!

ACKNOWLEDGEMENTS:

World War II, by H P Willmott/Robin Cross/
Charles Messenger

The Holy Bible (New International Version)

Fighting Aircraft of World War II, by Bill Gunston

The Lion Handbook to the Bible

Most Secret War, by R V Jones